Is Jeremy pushing himself too hard?

Keep going! a voice in Jeremy's head urged him. He was moving so fast, he was starting to feel a little dizzy. He was starting to see tiny black specks in the air in front of him, and his legs felt rubbery. His ears were ringing, too. But he was so close to the end. Just a few more down blocks and high blocks to go and he'd be done.

Just a few more moves, the voice in his head whispered . . .

The next thing he knew he was lying on the floor. Something cold and wet was being pressed against his forehead.

KARATE CLUB

High Pressure

CARIN GREENBERG BAKER

PUFFIN BOOKS

To my husband
Sensei David Baker

PUFFIN BOOKS
Published by the Penguin Group
Viking Penguin, a division of Penguin Books USA Inc.,
375 Hudson Street, New York, New York 10014, U.S.A.
Penguin Books Ltd, 27 Wrights Lane, London W8 5TZ, England
Penguin Books Australia Ltd, Ringwood, Victoria, Australia
Penguin Books Canada Ltd, 10 Alcorn Avenue, Toronto, Ontario, Canada M4V 3B2
Penguin Books (N.Z.) Ltd, 182–190 Wairau Road, Auckland 10, New Zealand

Penguin Books Ltd, Registered Offices: Harmondsworth, Middlesex, England

First published in the United States of America by Puffin Books,
a division of Penguin Books USA Inc., 1992
1 3 5 7 9 10 8 6 4 2

Copyright © KidsBooks, Inc., 1992
All rights reserved

Library of Congress Catalog Card Number: 91-68544
ISBN: 0-14-036025-5

Printed in the United States of America
Set in Bookman

He who is aware of his own weaknesses will remain master of himself in any situation.
—*Funakoshi*

Chapter One

"*In the way of the martial arts and their power, the preparation is all important. If the preparation has been sufficient, then the conclusion of the battle is inevitable.*"

—*Tokiyori*

Jeremy Jenkins sat on the floor of the Midvale Karate Dojo in *seiza* position. His legs were folded beneath him. His crossed hands rested lightly, palms up, on the knot of his green belt. His eyes were closed.

"Empty your mind of all thoughts," Sensei Davis's quiet, raspy voice directed Jeremy and the rest of the Monday afternoon karate class. *Sensei* was the Jap-

1

anese word for teacher. Sensei Davis was a third-degree black belt and the owner of the *dojo,* or school. "If a thought enters your head," Sensei told them, "gently push it away again."

Jeremy tried as hard as he could to relax his muscles and think of nothing. But his legs twitched with nervous energy and his mind kept filling with questions. When was Sensei going to clap his hands, signaling that class was over? Why had Sensei announced that there would be a *doshokai,* or meeting, right after class? Did the doshokai have anything to do with the upcoming karate demonstration?

The annual karate demonstration was the biggest event of the year. Students of all ranks and ages showed off their techniques. The audience was gigantic. Everyone in Midvale came, even the mayor! The demonstration was also covered by *The Courier,* Midvale's local newspaper.

It was important to do well in the demonstration, not just because so many people were watching, but also because it showed spirit. In karate, having a good attitude was just as important as having good technique. "Just like in everyday life," Sensei liked to remind them.

Jeremy had plenty of spirit, and he couldn't wait to prove it. He'd earned his green belt. Now he could play a much bigger part in the demonstration than last year, when he was just a white belt.

Sensei Davis clapped his hands once, loudly.

Jeremy opened his eyes and found himself staring at his brother Michael's back. Even sitting in seiza, Michael looked tall for a thirteen year old. His shoulders were broad, and he sat very straight. His hair, usually blond, looked much darker because it was still sweaty after the exercise of class. Michael, a green belt with brown tips, was one level more advanced than Jeremy.

Ahead of Michael in the row were several more colored belts. Behind Jeremy were some of the white belts. To Jeremy's left was a second line of students also ranked from back to front. Jeremy's other brother Lee, a brown belt, was at the head of that line because he was the most advanced student in the class.

Sensei knelt at the front of the classroom, facing the two lines. A sturdily built man in his late thirties, he had a sandy-colored mustache that matched his straight hair. Without getting up, Sensei turned to face the wall behind him. Hanging on the wall was a row of black and white photographs of the *shinden,* karate masters. Sensei's picture was at the far right, on the end. Beneath the photographs were the flags of Japan and the United States.

"Shinden ni rei," Sensei said, the signal for every-one to bow to the photographs. This showed respect for the teachers who'd come before them. Then Sensei turned back to face the class and motioned to Lee.

Small and wiry, Lee had straight black hair and almond-shaped brown eyes. Though Lee was twelve years old, a year older than Jeremy, they were both in sixth grade at Midvale Middle School. That was because Lee, a Vietnamese orphan, had been adopted by the Jenkins family when he was six years old. Since he hadn't spoken any English when he came to the United States, he'd had to start school in kindergarten instead of first grade.

Lee had introduced his brothers to karate. It was he who discovered the Midvale Karate Dojo, tucked between Plaza Shoes and Vinnie's Pizza at the local mall. Lee had started there first, then Michael, then Jeremy. Now all three of them were dedicated to the martial arts and they trained hard, several times a week.

"Dozo," Sensei said to Lee, meaning *please*.

"Sensei ni rei," Lee shouted, and everyone bowed to Sensei.

"Arigato, Sensei!" everyone said loudly, thanking him for teaching the class.

"Arigato!" Sensei thanked them back. In karate,

the teacher also learned from the student, which was why the teacher thanked the students, too.

Finally! Class was over. Now Jeremy would find out if Sensei was going to let him perform in the karate demonstration. Jeremy had volunteered to do *Pinan Shodan,* the first green belt *kata.* A kata was a series of carefully choreographed moves—blocks, punches, and kicks—usually done against an imaginary opponent. In this case, though, Jeremy was hoping to perform *Pinan Shodan bunkai*—meaning kata against *real* opponents. Lee and Michael had volunteered to be the opponents, along with Dwight Vernon, another friend from class.

Pinan Shodan was more advanced than the white belt kata, and Jeremy had only just begun to learn it. Still, he was confident he'd be ready to perform it in time for the demonstration. He only hoped Sensei felt the same way. Jeremy looked at Sensei expectantly.

Sensei gazed back, his dark brown eyes warm and peaceful. "We'll have a quick sweepdown of the deck," Sensei said. "Then everyone please form a circle." Sensei rose and disappeared behind the curtain leading to his office.

Barefoot, Jeremy and the other students raced to the broom closet at the back of the classroom, dodging

5

the occasional bucket collecting drips from the leaky ceiling. Jeremy grabbed a broom and started sweeping up the dusty wooden floor as fast as he could. In his haste, he nearly knocked over one of the buckets onto another pair of bare feet.

"Whoa!" joked Dwight Vernon, backing away as Jeremy stooped to steady the bucket. "Sensei said *sweep* the deck, not *mop* it! What's the rush?"

Jeremy looked up, embarrassed, into Dwight's grinning face. Dwight, a muscular thirteen year old, was in eighth grade. Dwight's black hair was razor cut very short, and his amber eyes stood out sharply against his brown skin. Like Michael, Dwight had a green belt with brown tips. Dwight's father, Vic Vernon, was a news reporter for the local television station, WMID-TV.

"Sorry," Jeremy said. "I just can't wait to find out if Sensei's going to let us do bunkai at the demonstration. I figured the faster I sweep, the faster we'll have the doshokai."

"Not if you start a flood," Dwight said. "We'd just have more work before it." His eyes twinkled as he said this, though, and Jeremy knew he was just teasing.

"Shhh!" said Rosalie Davis, a brown belt, who was sweeping nearby. "No talking on the deck." Rosalie was twelve years old—and Sensei's daughter. Like him, she had sandy hair and dark brown eyes. She'd been out with an injury the past few weeks, and she still wore a splint on her right hand. No one knew for sure, but the rumor was that she'd tried to break a brick with her fist. Jeremy could easily believe it because Rosalie did things like that all the time. She was hot-headed and always trying to prove how strong she was.

Sensei emerged from his office. "*Shotu-mate!*" he said, telling them to stop what they were doing. "Make a circle for doshokai."

Jeremy hastily swept his pile of dust into the center of the floor where Lee was waiting with a dustpan and whisk broom. Then Jeremy ran to the closet, replaced his broom, and ran back to the front of the room where students were already sitting on the floor in a circle. He found an empty spot in between his brothers.

All eyes turned to Sensei. He cleared his throat. "As I'm sure you know," he began, "we will be holding our annual karate demonstration in a few weeks. In the past, we've held it in the auditorium of Rosewood Elementary School, but there was never enough room for all the people who wanted to come. For this reason, Mayor Hernandez has given us permission to use the outdoor amphitheater on the town green. I'll be advertising in *The Courier* also. So this year I think we can expect a much larger audience than ever before. At least a few hundred people."

"Wow!" Jeremy whispered to Lee. "Big time!"

"There's something else that will be new this year," Sensei continued. "Vic Vernon, Dwight's dad, will be covering the event with his camera crew. We're going to be on television!"

An excited murmuring rose from the circle and Jeremy crossed his fingers on both hands. Now more than ever he hoped Sensei would allow him to do his bunkai. Jeremy pictured himself whipping around, powerfully, in low cat stance, effortlessly knocking down his opponents while the TV cameras followed his every move. Maybe he'd even get discovered! Maybe some movie producer would see him on the news and fly him to Hollywood to be the next Bruce Lee! He'd be famous. And rich. He smiled just thinking about it.

Sensei looked down at the clipboard balanced on his knees. "Unfortunately," he said, "more people volunteered for individual demonstrations than we'll have room for. But don't be discouraged if you weren't chosen. You'll still be able to participate in group kata."

Jeremy felt his heart plunge down to his belt. Had Sensei been looking at him, specifically, when he said that? What did this mean? Had Jeremy come this close to stardom only to have it taken away? It wasn't fair!

"I'll start with the white belts," Sensei said. "All of you will perform the first kata as a group. Green belt Jon Walker will demonstrate prearranged fighting numbers one and two with his sister, Alyse. Alyse will then join the other brown belts, Lee Jenkins and Rosalie Davis, to perform the *sai* kata."

The sai was a slender, pointed weapon with a U-shaped handle, used to defend against attacks with swords or blades. While karate literally meant "empty hand" and didn't involve much fighting with weapons, advanced students could choose to study a weapon. Some of the other weapons were the *bo,* a long wooden staff with tapered ends, and *nunchuku,* two wooden sticks, connected by a rope, which could be swung around like a flail. Jeremy couldn't wait until he was a brown belt, so he could choose a weapon. But right now he was a lot more worried about what Sensei Davis was going to say next.

Jeremy held his breath as Sensei looked over his list one more time. *Please say yes. Please say yes,* he prayed. It just wouldn't be fair if Jeremy had to stand on the sidelines while everyone else had a turn in the spotlight.

"Finally," Sensei said, pointing to something on his clipboard, "green belt Jeremy Jenkins will demonstrate Pinan Shodan bunkai with his brothers, Michael and Lee, and Dwight Vernon."

Jeremy couldn't suppress a yelp of delight, and he felt Michael and Lee slap him on the back in congratulations. On the other side of the circle, Dwight winked and gave him the thumbs up.

"Before you get too excited," Sensei said, fixing his gaze on Jeremy, "please remember that each of you will be completely responsible for your own demonstrations. You'll have to make your own arrangements to practice, either before or after class, or at home. I won't be supervising you, so plan your time accordingly. This is more than a chance to show your skills. It can also prove how responsible you are."

Sensei rose to his feet, and the class did the same. "Arigato, Sensei!" everyone shouted as they bowed.

"Arigato!" Sensei said, once more pushing through the curtain leading to his office.

As soon as Sensei was gone, Jeremy leaped into the air. "We made it!" he crowed to his brothers, slapping their hands in a high five. "This is going to be great!"

Dwight ambled across the room to join in the celebration. "We may not be as good as Bruce Lee," he said, "but at least we might end up on TV."

"Good going," Michael told him. "I know you must've had something to do with that."

"I just hope we'll have enough time to practice," Lee said soberly.

"Relax," Jeremy told him. "The demonstration's not for two weeks. There's plenty of time."

"Yeah, but you haven't been doing Pinan Shodan very long," Lee pointed out.

"Plus don't forget the science fair," Michael added.

"No sweat," Jeremy said. "I've got it *wired*."

"I hope so," Dwight said, "because I have it from an inside source that our bunkai could be *prominently* featured in my dad's piece."

Jeremy laughed. "You just tell your dad to keep the camera focused on *me*. Because when I get up there on that stage, I'm going to be *awesome*."

Chapter Two

"By now," said Miss Wilson, the eighth-grade science teacher, "I'm sure you are all well along in your projects for the county science fair. Many of you have discussed your ideas with me, and I must say I've been very impressed."

It was Tuesday, after school, and Jeremy sat in the back row of Miss Wilson's classroom. It was the second meeting for students competing in the upcoming fair. Miss Wilson was the science fair advisor for all the middle school students. She also happened to be Michael's science teacher. A trim, black woman in her mid-thirties, she usually wore no-nonsense clothes topped by a white lab coat. She dressed like a scientist. Now she stood behind the long counter at the front of the room, leaning forward on her elbows. A pair of brown horn-rimmed glasses dangled from a gold chain around her neck.

"The science fair," Miss Wilson continued, "will be held at the civic center and will include students from all the junior high schools in Dorchester County. The day will be broken up into two parts. In the morning, you will be assigned a booth in which to display your science project. The judges will come around to each booth to inspect your project and ask questions. Then, in the afternoon, you will each make a formal three-minute presentation to the judges and audience in the auditorium. Three finalists will be chosen, and I'm sure I don't need to remind you the winner will receive a five-thousand-dollar college scholarship before going on to the state competition. Any questions?"

A blonde girl sitting in front of Jeremy timidly raised her hand.

"Yes, Sandy?" Miss Wilson said.

Sandy, who'd been nibbling on her pen, quickly put it down. "Um . . . well . . . the subjects of my experiment . . . my gerbils, I mean, are kind of shy. I'm not sure how they'll perform in front of a large audience . . . ."

Blah, blah, blah, Jeremy thought. He'd known

13

Sandy since kindergarten, and he knew what her science project was. It was the same project she'd done the last two years at the elementary school science fair. Sandy was trying to teach her gerbils trained responses. It was kind of boring, though, because her gerbils were incredibly stupid. Either that, or Sandy wasn't a very good trainer. All Jeremy knew was that he'd never seen either of the furry guys do anything but curl up and sleep.

As Miss Wilson tried to answer Sandy's question, Jeremy looked around the classroom, checking out the rest of the competition. There was Rob Smith, a small-for-his-age seventh grader with braces. He was trying to create a new kind of sneakers with special rubber soles that allowed people to jump higher. Next to him sat Eddie Garcia, an eighth grader, who was working on a vacuum cleaner that could climb stairs by itself.

Jeremy tried not to smile. These people were no competition. None of these projects even came close to his.

Miss Wilson's classroom with its microscopes and petri dishes and sour smell of formaldehyde faded away as Jeremy's mind wandered. He imagined himself onstage, bowing to thunderous applause. His red hair, for once, was neatly combed. His wire-rimmed glasses reflected the brilliant glare of the spotlights, making him look . . . no, not nerdy. Cool and unreadable. Yeah! A distinguished old man in a gray suit walked onto the stage, bearing a silver trophy and a suitcase full of cash which he handed to Jeremy. The applause continued. People stood and whistled.

Then, Jeremy saw the front page of *The Courier:* KARATE KID KICKS OUT THE COMPETITION AT SCIENCE FAIR blared the headline. Beneath it, side by side, were two photographs. One was an action pose of Jeremy in his *gi,* sending Michael, Lee, *and* Dwight flying through the air with his powerful front snap kick. The other featured a smiling Jeremy, counting his money.

"Jeremy Jenkins, a powerhouse with brains and brawn," said the smooth, deep voice of Vic Vernon, sitting in the studio of WMID-TV with Jeremy beside him. "Tell me, Jeremy," Vic said, "what is the secret of your success?"

Jeremy, wearing his gi and holding his silver trophy, shrugged modestly. "I guess I was born this way, Vic. I've always done well without even trying."

"Is it true," Vic asked, "that there will soon be a comic book based on your life?"

Jeremy nodded. "As I'm sure everyone in America knows, my mother is editor-in-chief of Rocket Comics and creator of the famous superhero, Turbotron."

"Of course," Vic said. "Turbotron has the brilliant mind of a computer, the brave heart of a human, and superhuman strength from his internal turbo-charged engine."

"Exactly," said Jeremy. "Well, now my mother's decided that a character based on me will be even *more* popular!"

"Jeremy!" Vic shouted. "Jeremy Jenkins! Are you listening to me?"

"Of course I'm listening," Jeremy said, starting to get confused.

"Jeremy, I said the meeting's over. You can go home now."

Vic Vernon's face evaporated and Jeremy saw a pair of brown horn-rimmed glasses dangling on a chain in front of his eyes. Jeremy looked up into the kind face of Miss Wilson, who was leaning over his desk. Behind her, a few students were gathering their books. Some were already heading out the door.

"Did you want to speak to me privately about your project?" Miss Wilson asked. "I don't think we've discussed it yet, have we?"

"Uh . . . no," Jeremy said. "But I've got it all under control. I don't need any help or anything."

Actually, Jeremy hadn't started building his project yet. He hadn't even bought the materials. But those were technicalities. What counted was the idea. And Jeremy had a great one.

"Well, if you need me, you know where to find me," Miss Wilson said, turning around and heading to the front of the classroom where two students were waiting to talk to her.

Though it was nice of Miss Wilson to offer her services, Jeremy knew he'd be able to handle this project on his own. After all, he'd won first place in his elementary school science fair last year with his environmental awareness project. He had designed a really cool mini-ecosystem in an old aquarium, complete with plants and "animals"—insects, actually. Now he was a whole year older and smarter. Winning this competition was going to be a snap!

Whistling a happy tune, Jeremy grabbed his denim jacket off the back of his chair and headed for the door. Just before he left, he heard something that made him pause.

"This is wonderful!" Miss Wilson exclaimed. Her glasses now sat low on her nose, and she was examining several large sheets of white paper laid out on the long black counter that was her desk. "Really, truly original. And very clever."

Standing next to Miss Wilson, a tall, slender girl with curly light brown hair smiled proudly. Jeremy knew the girl. She was Suzanne Whittaker. Like Michael, she was in Miss Wilson's eighth-grade science class. She was also the twin sister of *Jason* Whittaker, the school football star who'd gotten into a big fight with Lee last week.

Lee had beaten Jason easily. Jeremy hadn't been so lucky, though, when he'd tangled with Jason a few days before. Jason had given Jeremy a fat lip and busted his glasses.

It was true the feud was over, but Jeremy always hated losing. The last thing he wanted was to be beaten by *another* Whittaker. Chances were, he had nothing to worry about. Suzanne couldn't have a better idea than he did. But it couldn't hurt to keep an eye—and ear—on the competition.

Pretending to study the yellowing periodic table of elements thumbtacked to the wall, Jeremy strained to hear more of Miss Wilson's conversation with Suzanne.

"Of course it's not finished yet," Suzanne was saying, "but I did a test run in the basement, and I think it's going to work once I iron out a few of the kinks."

Miss Wilson nodded. "It's an ambitious project. These diagrams are quite sophisticated for someone your age. I'm very impressed."

Jeremy felt like throwing up. Suzanne was obviously going out of her way to suck up to Miss Wilson. Miss Wilson was just as bad though, falling all over Suzanne.

What could Suzanne possibly have done that could get Miss Wilson so excited? Jeremy had to find out. It might mean being a little late to meet Michael and Lee by the bike rack, but they'd still have enough time to get to the dojo, and Jeremy was sure his brothers would understand.

Out of the corner of his eye, Jeremy saw that Suzanne was rolling up her diagrams. Miss Wilson was already talking with another student. Hoping Suzanne hadn't noticed him standing there, Jeremy slipped out into the hallway and took a long sip of water from the drinking fountain. When Suzanne came out into the hallway, he could pretend he'd just happened to run into her.

"Suzanne!" Jeremy called, wiping the icy water from his mouth. "Wait up!"

Suzanne looked up and smiled. Jeremy could see books and the rolled sheets of paper sticking out of her backpack. "Hi, Jeremy," she said, her green eyes sparkling. "How's your science project going?"

Now that he was close enough to actually talk to Suzanne, Jeremy felt tongue-tied. She was, after all, a girl. And Jeremy still felt embarrassed that he'd accused Suzanne of spying for her brothers when Jason and Kevin were feuding with Lee and him. Kevin, in the sixth grade with Jeremy and Lee, was also a white belt in their karate class.

"Uh . . . fine," Jeremy muttered as they started walking together down the hall. "How's yours?"

"I'm really happy with it," Suzanne said. "I've been working really hard on it a long time, but it's finally coming together."

"What is it, exactly?" Jeremy asked casually, looking down at his sneakers so she couldn't see the eagerness in his face.

"I'd rather not talk about it," Suzanne said. "I haven't told anyone except my family and Miss Wilson."

"I wouldn't tell anybody," Jeremy said, "or steal your idea, or anything. I already know what I'm doing."

"It's nothing personal," Suzanne said. "I just don't want to talk about it until it's ready. You know what

I mean, don't you? I mean, do you want to talk about yours?"

No, Jeremy thought, *because I don't have a project yet. At least, nothing you could see.* But that wasn't really true. Jeremy *did* have a project, in his mind. So what if he hadn't spent every night holed up in his room just to get it built two weeks ahead of time? The important thing was to have it ready for the science fair. Jeremy could do that, no sweat.

Suzanne readjusted the straps on her backpack. "Well, I've got to get home to work on my project. See you around." With a quick wave, she headed off.

Jeremy was tempted to run after her and pluck the diagrams from her bag. But that was stupid. What difference did it make what Suzanne was doing? The important thing was his project. And with the science fair less than two weeks away, he had to start working on it *soon.*

Chapter Three

"What took you?" Michael wanted to know as Jeremy raced up the concrete walk behind the school. He and Lee stood with their ten speeds near the bicycle rack. "We were just about to leave without you."

"Sorry," Jeremy said, his face flushed from running. "The science fair meeting took too long." That was sort of the truth. Jeremy grabbed his bike chain and spun the combination on his lock. "Look, I'm ready to go. We won't even be late. You'll see."

A few minutes later, they were coasting down the hill towards the mall. Nearly half a mile long, the mall had every kind of store and fast-food restaurant, plus a twelve-plex movie theater. All the stores were connected by a covered walkway. It wasn't as fancy as the enclosed mall just outside town with its electric walkway and fountains, but it was Jeremy's favorite because it had the dojo, *and* a fantastic video arcade.

Weaving through parked cars, the boys glided right up to the Midvale Karate Dojo and locked their bikes to the rack. The dojo had a big glass window, and a red satin banner hung inside it, facing out. Embroidered on the banner was a large gold circle with a clenched fist over crossed sai.

"See?" Jeremy said, pointing to his watch as he followed his brothers through the glass door of the dojo. "It's only quarter after. Class doesn't start for another fifteen minutes."

"Yeah, but we wanted to practice our bunkai before class," Lee said as he sat down on a rough-hewn wooden bench in the front hall. The hall ran from left to right and had windows starting halfway up so visitors could look into the classroom beyond. "Now we'll have to do it after, because it will be too late by the time we get changed." Lee's straight black hair fell in front of his eyes as he leaned down to unlace his sneakers. Michael sat beside him and did the same. Jeremy didn't bother to sit down but simply stepped on the heels of his sneakers and kicked them off. Shoes weren't allowed inside the classroom.

Placing their shoes on shelves inside a closet on the right wall, the boys passed through a curtained doorway leading to the classroom, or deck. It was a large,

23

square room. The left wall, with its flags and photographs of the ancient masters, was actually the front of the classroom.

The floor, made of polished wood, was slightly warped in places from the leaky ceiling. Every time Sensei had a leak fixed, a new leak would spring up. Sensei liked to say the dojo was blessed by the Japanese water god. Jeremy used to believe this until Lee told him there *was* no Japanese water god.

There were already half a dozen *deshi,* karate students, warming up on the deck. Some white belts were practicing the first kata, watching their movements in the mirrors mounted on the side walls. Rosalie Davis, Sensei's daughter, stood near the back wall, punching the *makiwara* with her left hand. The makiwara was a wooden beam, about four feet high, mounted in the floor. The top of it had rope wrapped around it. Deshi punched the roped part to toughen their knuckles and their fists.

"*Hyaaaaah!*" Rosalie yelled each time her fist hit the makiwara. This yell was called *kiai*, a focusing of energy and power in one sharp burst.

"If she's not careful, she's going to have a cast on her *left* hand too," Lee joked.

Bowing to the flags and photographs as was customary, the Jenkins brothers walked across the deck and bowed again before entering the boys' dressing room. The room was plain, with a wooden floor, gray metal lockers, and a single wooden bench. There was also a sink, toilet, and shower at one end.

"So how's your science project going?" Michael asked Jeremy as they started to undress. "You haven't talked too much about it."

"I've got it all worked out," Jeremy said, stepping into the white cotton pants of his gi. "I've got the sketches all drawn, and I've figured out everything I need to buy. All I have to do now is buy the parts and put it together."

"What exactly *is* your project?" Lee asked, tying the strings of his gi shirt closed.

Jeremy put a finger to his lips. He peeked inside the shower stall and behind the curtain that hid the toilet. Then he poked his head out onto the deck and checked to see if anyone was standing near the locker room.

"What are you doing?" Lee asked.

"It's a secret!" Jeremy whispered. "I don't want anyone to hear, especially Kevin Whittaker." Kevin, a white belt, was the younger brother of Suzanne and Jason. If Suzanne wasn't going to reveal what *she* was

25

doing, Jeremy didn't want her to know his idea either.

"Kevin's out on the deck doing kata," Michael said. "So come on, tell."

"OK," Jeremy said, sitting down on the wooden bench. His brothers, both tying on their colored belts, moved closer to listen. "I invented a working model of the solar system." He paused, allowing his brilliance to sink in, but seeing his brothers' confusion, he continued. "You know how the planets rotate on their axes and revolve around the sun?" Jeremy asked.

Michael and Lee nodded.

"Well, I've figured out a system of gears that will allow me to make miniature planets that can rotate and revolve at the same time! It's hard to describe, but you'll see it when I'm done."

"Sounds pretty good," Lee said.

"But that's not the great part," Jeremy said. "Not only will my planets rotate and revolve, but they'll move at the correct speeds relative to each other! Like, Earth and Mars will rotate at around the same speed, but Pluto will rotate about four times faster. So what I've really done is invented a new way to control speed and motion. I'm sure there are lots of commercial applications for it. Maybe I'll even get a patent!"

26

Michael smiled and punched Jeremy's arm. "Not bad for a squirt!"

"Just don't forget us when you're a rich and famous inventor," Lee said. "You can invite us over to your mansion to swim in your pool."

"I'll buy you your *own* mansions," Jeremy bragged. "This invention's just the beginning."

"I just hope you have time to practice our bunkai in between working on your brilliant invention," Michael said. "We have a lot of work to do in the next two weeks."

"My own brother," Jeremy said, shaking his head. "Have I ever not come through? I always get good grades, right?"

"Uh-huh," Michael said, slamming his locker shut.

"Am I a totally awesome Ninja warrior or what?"

"Totally," Lee said as they pushed through the curtained doorway leading to the deck.

"Then *trust* me," Jeremy said. "I've got it all wired. I'm a natural!"

"*Shugo,* line up!" called Sensei, emerging from his office.

Bowing hastily to Sensei, the brothers ran to take their places.

One hour, one hundred deep knee bends, and several dozen kata later, the boys were back in the same two lines, bowing to Sensei as class ended. "Arigato, Sensei!" the class shouted.

As usual, Jeremy had pushed himself to the point of exhaustion. His gi was damp with sweat and his face was so warm his glasses were foggy. Hard as he had worked out, though, Jeremy still had plenty of energy left for Pinan Shodan. *And* his science project.

"Let's go!" Jeremy said to his brothers after Sensei had gone into his office. "Where's Dwight?"

"Right here," Dwight said, lifting his head from the drinking fountain which was recessed in the wall between the locker rooms. "You ready for a little three on one? Think you can handle us?"

"Just watch me," Jeremy said, finding an empty spot on the mat. He stood at attention, his heels touching, his toes turned out. His hands rested lightly at his sides.

Lee and Michael took ready stances to Jeremy's right and left, their fists raised at chest level, their elbows tucked in to their ribs. Dwight took a similar position behind Jeremy.

"Oh, wow, I'm scared," Jeremy joked.

"Do it half speed, half power," Lee directed, since he was the highest ranking student. "Let's just get the moves down. *Yo-i!*" That was the command for Jeremy to take the ready position.

28

Jeremy bowed, then took a wide stance, holding his arms straight down in front of him, hands clenched into fists.

"*Hajime!*" Lee gave the command to begin.

In slow motion, Michael, to Jeremy's left, threw a punch at Jeremy's face. Jeremy dropped down into cat stance, putting all his weight on his bent back leg and resting the ball of his front foot lightly on the floor. At the same time, he blocked his chest and face with a twisting motion of his arms, deflecting Michael's fist. He waited, his right arm up in high block, his left arm blocking his chest.

Michael then punched to Jeremy's chest, which Jeremy blocked by dropping his right arm with a twisting motion against Michael's arm. Then Jeremy counterattacked with a left punch to Michael's solar plexus. The solar plexus was the nerve center right beneath the rib cage. If you landed a good shot there, you could disable your opponent. But of course this was just half speed and power, which meant Jeremy barely touched Michael. The object was to get the moves down, not to hurt each other.

Lee, from Jeremy's other side, came at him with a walking chest punch, which Jeremy also flung away with a double block in cat stance. Lee grabbed Jeremy's right arm, but Jeremy broke the hold by drop-

29

ping his left arm and countering with a right punch to the solar plexus.

Dwight, behind Jeremy, aimed a chasing punch at Jeremy's ribs. Jeremy turned towards Dwight with a chest block, then aimed a front snap kick at Dwight's solar plexus.

Meanwhile, Michael had moved around to Jeremy's back, ready to attack again. Too fast, Jeremy whipped around to face Michael in cat stance, and he wobbled.

"Sorry," Jeremy said. "These turns in cat stance are a little tricky."

"Slow down," Lee advised. "Get familiar with the footwork so you know where you're going."

Jeremy blocked three walking punches from Michael, then turned in cat stance to block Dwight and Lee's punches coming at him from the left and right.

"Get lower!" Lee instructed. "Really bend that back leg!"

Jeremy's legs were tired from an hour of deep knee bends and practicing Pinan Shodan in his class, but he wouldn't give up. Soon, Jeremy's legs were shaking so hard from the strain he thought he'd fall over. "This cat stance is really tough!" Jeremy said. "Let's knock it off, okay? We've been practicing long enough. If I

30

break my legs practicing, it won't do much good."

"Already?" Dwight asked. "It's only quarter to five!"

"Quarter to five?" Jeremy looked up at the clock on the wall above the drinking fountain. "I almost forgot! I have to get to the hardware store before they close. I've got to buy some gears for my project."

Lee sighed and shook his head. "We haven't made very much progress. This is the worst time to stop. You should practice until you get it right, and then keep doing it awhile to get it down smooth." Lee was very dedicated; that's why he was the best.

Jeremy looked pleadingly at his brothers. "Look, I'll practice at home tonight," he said, "and we can work again tomorrow after class. But the hardware store closes at five. If I don't leave now, I'll never make it."

"Go ahead," Michael said, shrugging. "We'll meet you at home."

"Thanks," Jeremy said. "I swear I'll be able to work a lot longer tomorrow."

With barely a bow to the flags, Jeremy rushed into the locker room, flung his sweaty gi into his locker, pulled on his jeans and T-shirt, and shoved one arm through the sleeve of his jacket. With the other sleeve flapping in the wind, Jeremy pedaled furiously down the sidewalk, dodging pedestrians and grocery carts as he headed for Chuck's Hardware.

"Whew!" Jeremy said as he opened the door of the hardware store. His watch showed five minutes to five.

"We're closing," a middle-aged man behind the counter told Jeremy.

"I know exactly what I want," Jeremy said breathlessly, rummaging inside the pocket of his jeans for the list he'd made. It was in there somewhere. Jeremy pulled out some change, a crumpled tissue, and a pencil stub before he found the wadded-up piece of paper. Unfolding it, he glanced over it quickly. He needed five different sizes of gears, nine three-volt motors, metal rods, and nylon cord.

"Four minutes," the man warned.

Jeremy took off, running on shaky legs down the center aisle. His lungs were burning and it felt painful to breathe, but he didn't dare stop. He passed light bulbs, hammers, nails, fifteen kinds of glue, drill bits, ironing board covers, and rubber bathmats, but he couldn't find anything on his list.

"Hey!" Jeremy said, careening into the front counter where the man stood behind the cash register, pulling on his coat. "Can you help me find some of this stuff?" He thrust his list at the man, who took it reluctantly.

The man started shaking his head as soon as he read the piece of paper. "You got the wrong kind of store," he said. "You want a hobby store. We don't carry any of this stuff."

"Is there a store like that nearby?" Jeremy asked, looking anxiously at his watch. "I need this stuff right away."

The man shook his head again and started buttoning his jacket. "The only one I know of is Universal Hobbies and Crafts, but that's on the other side of town."

"Can I go over there now?"

"They close at five," the man said, leaning over to the wall to turn out some fluorescent lights in the back of the store. "Just like me."

Jeremy felt like kicking his way out the door, but he forced himself to use the doorknob. He'd have to go to Universal tomorrow, but that would mean missing karate *and* their next bunkai practice session. Jeremy wasn't looking forward to telling his brothers. Jeremy hopped on his bike and pedaled back towards the dojo. Michael and Jeremy were still outside, talking to Dwight.

"How'd it go?" Michael asked as Jeremy squeezed his hand brakes and stopped. "Did they have what you were looking for?"

"Uh . . . not exactly," Jeremy said, biting his lip.

"What does that mean?" Lee asked, studying Jeremy's face.

"It means I have to go to a different store. I won't be able to make it to the dojo tomorrow," Jeremy said quickly, looking off at the parking lot so he wouldn't have to see their reactions. He had to make it up to them, somehow. "I know!" he said suddenly. "I can practice with you guys tomorrow when we all get home. We've worked out in the basement before." Jeremy and his brothers had set up a mini-dojo in the basement of their house. Since they were always practicing down there, their dad had nicknamed the three boys "The Karate Club."

"That's fine for us, maybe," Michael said, "but what about Dwight? Maybe *he's* not available."

"Well," Dwight said, "I have a meeting with the President tomorrow, but I'll see if I can rearrange my schedule."

Jeremy laughed. "Tell the President it will never happen again."

"Do you think you can get home by five o'clock?"

34

Lee asked. "That would give us an hour or so before dinner."

"No sweat," Jeremy said. "I'll go to the store right after school. I'll be home before you."

Dwight's mother pulled up in front of the dojo in her station wagon. Dwight's dog, Betty, a white shaggy mutt, was sitting in the front seat next to Mrs. Vernon. Betty paced and turned excitedly when she saw Dwight, then hung her scraggly head out the open window.

"Well, see you guys tomorrow," Dwight said.

"See you!" Jeremy called after him. "Five o'clock on the nose."

Chapter Four

Ker-plonk!

Every time Jeremy rode over a pothole in the bumpy road, his heavy backpack came pounding down between his shoulder blades with a painful . . .

Ker-plonk!

Thirty pounds of metal filled the olive-green canvas with sharp bulges that poked through his denim jacket and made his back ache. It felt like a hundred pounds of thorns. Jeremy tried to ignore the pain and concentrate on pumping the pedals of his bicycle. The problem was, no matter how fast he pedaled, it wasn't fast enough.

Ker-plonk! The jabbing pains were just a reminder of how late he was. It was five forty-five Wednesday afternoon, and Jeremy was nowhere near home where his brothers and Dwight had been waiting to practice bunkai with him. When Jeremy had set out to find Universal Hobbies and Crafts after school, he'd had no idea how far away it was. It had taken him nearly an hour to get there. He should have looked at a map, maybe even called ahead of time.

The good news was that the store had had everything he needed to build his model of the solar system. Jeremy had spent a month's worth of allowance, buying gears in every size, cogs, screws, metal rods, nylon cord, and nine three-volt battery-operated motors, which he'd tucked inside his pack. In fact, he might still have been on time if he'd gone straight home.

Then he'd passed an art supply store on the way home. So, to save himself an extra trip later, he decided to stop there, too.

All Jeremy needed were a few cans of enamel paint so he could paint his planets in realistic colors. But first he went through all the aisles looking for the paint before he realized he could just have looked—should just have looked—at the directory signs that hung over each aisle. Then he got stuck on a really long line. By the time he left, it was already five o'clock.

Ker-plonk! Now here he was, clanking and rattling like a rusty old car, soaked in sweat, and it felt like his back was being hammered. Worst of all, it was almost six o'clock. He'd missed nearly the whole practice session.

Jeremy pedaled onto his street, a wide, tree-lined avenue with large houses. He skidded through piles of red and brown leaves, damp from the recent rain. The road narrowed and twisted and became a dead end.

The Jenkins house was the last house on the right. Half-hidden behind bushes and trees, it was over a hundred years old, made of stone, with a woods behind it. A modern, wood-shingled, two-car garage had been added. Both garage doors were open now, and Jeremy saw that his dad's Jeep and his mom's sportscar were in their usual places. That meant he'd have to face his parents as well as his brothers when he walked in the door. This was going to be ugly. Jeremy parked his bike inside the garage and opened the door leading to the kitchen.

Jeremy's dad, Stephen Jenkins, was bent over the open oven, his muscular arms inside. He straightened up, bearing a lasagna in a metal baking dish. Steam rose from the lasagna, fogging up his wire-rimmed glasses and causing his blond hair to stick to his forehead.

Jeremy's mother, Andrea, stood at the counter tossing a salad. Her curly red hair stood out all over her head like a copper halo. Small and slim, she wore a bright blue sweat suit that matched her eyes.

Michael and Lee sat at the table, staring silently at Jeremy as he stood in the doorway.

Jeremy dropped his heavy knapsack to the floor with a loud *klunk!* "Sorry I'm late," he said sheepishly. "I . . . I should have called, but the only phone I passed on the way was broken."

Michael and Lee continued to stare. Mrs. Jenkins looked up briefly from her salad, then looked down again. Jeremy knew exactly what that meant. It meant that she knew what the problem was but she was leaving it up to her sons to work it out for themselves. At least, that's what she *meant* to do, but she always ended up giving her opinion, sooner or later.

"I guess Dwight went home," Jeremy said, trying to break the silence and invite his brothers to start yelling at him. It wouldn't be pleasant, but at least that way they could get it over with.

"He couldn't wait any more," Michael said sternly. "We practiced bunkai in the basement, but it's pretty hard fighting someone who isn't there."

"Yeah," Lee said. "We get enough of fighting imaginary opponents when we do kata. The whole point of bunkai is to have a *real* opponent."

"I'm really, really sorry," Jeremy said. "The hobby store was farther away than I thought and the art store was really crowded. It's not like I did it on purpose."

"That's not the point," Michael said. "The point is, you *promised* you'd be home by five o'clock. No matter what problems you were having, you should have figured out a way to get here."

"That's right," Lee agreed. "You know what Sensei says. Whatever it takes, *just do it.*"

Jeremy started to protest, but then he thought back to how he'd waited on that long line at the art store. If he'd put the paints back instead, he could have made it home in time. Or maybe he should never have gone to the art store at all, since he was already so far from home.

"Is Dwight really mad?" Jeremy asked, taking his place at the table as his father carried the steaming lasagna over.

"He wasn't exactly jumping for joy," Michael said.

Mr. Jenkins loaded Jeremy's plate with a generous serving. The warm, sweet smell of tomatoes and melted mozzarella cheese wafted up. Usually, Jeremy couldn't wait to dig in his fork, but his stomach was twisted so tight he couldn't even think about eating.

What if Dwight told his father not to put them on the news because of what Jeremy did?

"Maybe you've taken on more than you can handle, Jeremy," said Mr. Jenkins, sitting down at one end of the table. "If you don't have time to do your science project *and* the karate, maybe you should give something up."

"I can handle it," Jeremy insisted. "I just needed to buy my materials, but now I've done all that. Now I have all the stuff, I'll be able to practice *whenever*."

"How about right after dinner?" Michael suggested. "We can make up for lost time."

"Sure," Jeremy said, trying not to think about the pack full of gears and equipment sitting by the garage door. He could begin building his model later in the evening.

"Good," Lee said. "Dwight won't be here, but we can work with him tomorrow after class."

"I can be Dwight *and* myself," Michael said. "That way I can practice the rest of the bunkai."

Now that his brothers seemed less angry, Jeremy could finally relax. He still felt bad, but his appetite returned. He managed to pack away two helpings of lasagna, three bowls of salad, four slices of bread, and a slab of chocolate cake before pushing himself back from the table. "OK," he told his brothers. "Let's go."

Lee and Michael jumped up and carried their dishes to the sink. Jeremy followed, then they all raced downstairs. The basement was unfinished, with cinder block walls and a cement floor. At one end were a washer and dryer and overhead racks for drying clothes. At the other end were a Ping-Pong table, a work bench, and several stacked cardboard boxes.

A large space had been cleared in the center to create a mini-dojo. Mr. Jenkins had attached several mirrors to one wall, and the boys had hung flags of the United States and Japan above them. Framed certificates, decorated with Japanese lettering, displayed the ranks they'd earned in karate, and Lee's sai crisscrossed each other on the wall. Also above the mirror was a large sign which said The Karate Club. Michael, who was a talented artist, had hand-lettered the sign.

Jeremy looked at his watch. It was almost seven o'clock. He had to go to bed by ten. That left just three hours to practice bunkai, do his homework, and start building his project. There was no time to waste. Jeremy stepped out of his sneakers and kicked them across the room. Then he stood in the center of the empty space, legs wide, fists clenched down in front of him. "I'm ready," he said.

"Let's do it half speed, half power again," Lee said, "since you still don't have the moves down and we're not warmed up yet."

"I do so!" Jeremy protested. "And I'm tired of doing it half speed. I want to do it full speed and power like we're going to do at the demonstration." *Besides*, thought Jeremy, *the faster the moves, the faster we get through this*.

"You're not going to have much power if you don't know what you're doing," Michael warned.

"And we're not going to get much practicing done if we stand here talking," Jeremy said, checking his watch again. It was five after seven.

"Take your watch off," Lee said. "You're not supposed to wear it during practice. Someone could get hurt."

"Sorry," Jeremy said, tossing the black, hard plastic watch on the Ping-Pong table. "Can we start now?"

"*Half* speed," Lee emphasized as he and Michael took their stances on either side of Jeremy. "Hajime!"

As Jeremy blocked Michael's punches, he realized how sore his neck and shoulders were from the heavy load he'd carried. His legs hurt, too, from two hours of pedaling to the hobby store and back. So far, his body hurt more from his science project than from doing bunkai!

Jeremy turned in cat stance to block Lee's foot, which was heading straight for his nose. "Hey!" Jeremy said, straightening up. "That wasn't the move you used last time. It was a walking punch."

Lee shook his head. "That's what bunkai is all about. In a real fight, you don't know how you'll be attacked, so you've got to be ready for anything."

"But this is supposed to be *choreographed*," Jeremy said. "If we don't practice it the same way every time, how am I supposed to look good on television?"

"Stop worrying about the TV cameras," Michael said. "Just concentrate on what you're doing."

Jeremy shut his mouth and made a quarter turn to his right to block Lee's chasing punch to his ribs. He *couldn't* forget about the TV cameras. Maybe he was foolish, though, to worry about looking good. Maybe Dwight was so angry he'd tell his father to make Jeremy look *bad*. Jeremy could hear Vic Vernon's voice narrating over the videotape as Jeremy failed to block a punch and went sprawling on the stage of the amphitheater: "Karate. An effective form of self-defense, but useless in the wrong hands. This is the sad story of Jeremy Jenkins. He was strong. He had potential.

But he made one serious mistake. He made my son mad . . ."

"Jeremy . . . " Lee's voice called him back to attention.

Jeremy realized he'd been staring into the blackness of Lee's T-shirt for several seconds. "Sorry," he said. "Where were we?"

"Front snap kick," Lee directed.

Jeremy pointed his toes at Lee's solar plexus, then whipped around in cat stance, his knife hands blocking Michael's walking punches to his chest.

"*Hayeeee!*" Jeremy kiai-ed, thrusting a spear hand into Michael's solar plexus. Like knife hands, spear hands had the fingers extended, stiff and straight and stuck together with the thumb tucked in tightly. The difference between knife hands and spear hands was in how they were used. Knife hands struck with the side of the hand, from pinkie to wrist. Spear hands struck with the tips of the fingers. Jeremy spun around and used knife hands to block Lee's punch to the chest.

As Jeremy continued turning, with his brothers circling him, he almost felt like the sun in his solar system model, the one he hadn't built yet. Jeremy thought again of the gears and cogs waiting for him upstairs and wondered what time it was. The first thing he

45

wanted to do was double-check his calculations to make sure he had the ratios right for his gears. Then he planned to mount the sun on a central shaft. Each planet would be attached to the central shaft by a metal rod which would be driven by a tiny, three-volt motor. The motor would be attached by . . .

A blur shot by his face, and he turned suddenly. Too suddenly. He toppled over, falling into Michael's legs and knocking him over as well.

"Jeremy!" Lee and Michael shouted together. Michael scrambled to his feet angrily, not even bothering to offer Jeremy a hand up.

"Uh-oh . . . " Jeremy looked around him. He couldn't remember how many times he'd shifted around in cat stance. His brothers were no longer poised to attack but simply stood there, glaring. "You want to start again?" Jeremy asked.

Before they could answer, their mother's voice called down to them from the kitchen. "Time to do your homework!" she shouted.

Jeremy jumped up and headed towards the Ping-Pong table to get his watch. "I know I'm a little distracted right now," he said, "but don't worry. I know Pinan Shodan perfectly. I just need a little polishing."

"More than a little," Michael said.

"However much I need, that's how much we'll do,"
Jeremy vowed, picking up his sneakers. "You'll see.
We're going to be the best! I promise!" Without waiting any longer, Jeremy raced up the stairs. He felt
bad about the bunkai, but he was relieved to finally
get to work on his science project. In the kitchen, he
hefted his knapsack up off the floor, then he went
straight upstairs to his room.

Jeremy's room was long and narrow, with a ceiling
that sloped down over his single bed. His bedspread
featured Turbotron, the superhero his mother had
created for Rocket Comics, where she worked. The
opposite wall of the room was lined with bookshelves,
with a desk sandwiched in between. The shelves were
loaded with science fiction paperbacks and thick
books about rocket ships and astronomy. Tacked up
on a bulletin board above his desk were scribbled
sketches of the solar system with columns of numbers
marching down the edges.

Jeremy dumped his backpack on his desk and
started unloading all his supplies. He had his own tool
chest in the closet. It was so tempting to start building
his model right now, but he had a ton of math homework to do first. Jeremy was in a special math program
for advanced students and they'd just started a new

unit on pre-algebra. Pushing aside the paint cans and gears, Jeremy opened his textbook and switched on his desk lamp.

By the time Jeremy had finished his homework, it was ten minutes to ten. There was no time left to start his project, or even to practice Pinan Shodan. It was time to go wash up, and Jeremy was starting to feel a little guilty. He hadn't gotten nearly as much done as he'd planned.

But maybe he was being too hard on himself. He had bought every single thing he needed to build his project, hadn't he? He also had practiced his kata, hadn't he? And it was only Wednesday. He still had a week and three days until the science fair, and a week and *four* days until the demonstration. He was still in good shape. In fact, he was practically golden. It was a lock!

After he brushed his teeth and washed his face and said good night to his parents, Jeremy climbed into bed. He was too tired to move, and his back hurt from his long bike trip. His chest felt tight, too, and it was a little hard to breathe deeply. But Jeremy wasn't worried. It was probably overall muscle soreness. He'd feel much better in the morning.

Chapter Five

"Hey, gimme my banana!" someone shouted, Thursday afternoon, at the lunch table behind Lee. "Give it!"

"Catch!" someone else yelled meanly as the banana, dark yellow with large black splotches on it, whizzed past Lee's ear.

A boy barreled past Lee's table, his hands reaching up to catch the banana, like a wide receiver going for a big play. He wasn't looking where he was going, and he slammed into a garbage can, knocking it over.

"Hey!" bellowed Mr. Rosario, the lunchroom monitor. "Settle down over there!"

Lee closed his eyes and ignored the yells and the smells of the cafeteria. Michael and Jeremy had just gone to buy lunch, so Lee had a few moments alone. He wanted to think about karate. The big demonstration was only a week and three days away, not a long time. Lee planned to use every free second he had between now and then mentally preparing for his part in it.

Lee would be performing the sai kata, a series of choreographed moves with two metal weapons that looked like short swords. Lee knew the kata backwards and forwards, but he was still worried about his technique. There was one move where he had to spin both sai around very fast, keeping them as close to his forearms as possible. Lee still wasn't happy with the way he did this move. He wasn't doing it fast enough, and the sai kept wobbling out to the side. It was important to be smooth. Smooth and perfect.

Lee tried to visualize himself doing it, his wrists flicking in rapid figure eights as the sai whipped around and around. Lee moved his wrists back and forth, faster and faster, trying to imagine the weight of the cold swords in his hands.

"What are you doing?" a voice asked. "Conducting an orchestra?"

Lee opened his eyes, embarrassed. The blood rushed to his face. When he saw who was talking, though, his heart started pumping faster.

Staring down at him, huge in his red and white football jersey, was Jason Whittaker. Jason was the star quarterback on the football team. He was also the guy who'd picked a fight with Lee the week before, after the Friday game. Jason had the height and weight advantage, but luckily he'd been no match for Lee's advanced karate techniques.

They'd talked, afterwards, and sort of straightened things out, but they hadn't talked since then. Lee wasn't sure if Jason was being friendly—or trying to pick another fight.

Lee stared up at Jason warily. "I was thinking about a move for our karate demonstration," he said. "I guess I got carried away." He studied Jason for the anger he'd seen last week, but all he saw was curly brown hair and a broad ruddy face with green eyes that looked almost . . . friendly.

Jason noded. "My brother Kevin told me about it," he said. "He's really excited, too, 'cause he gets to do the first . . . I forget the word."

"Kata," Lee said. "It's the first thing you learn when you're a white belt. It's basically a lot of walking punches and high blocks and low blocks."

"I know," Jason said. "Kevin's practiced it so many times in the backyard that I can almost do it myself just from watching him. But I'm sure it's not as advanced as what you're doing."

This conversation wasn't turning out the way Lee

51

had expected at all. Jason seemed to be going out of his way to make conversation, and he seemed genuinely interested in karate. Lee let his guard down, a little.

"My brothers are going to be in the demonstration, too," Lee said. "We're doing a mock fight. It's called bunkai."

Jason shifted from one sneakered foot to the other. He looked like he wanted to keep talking, but he didn't know what to say.

Lee didn't know what to say either. It was one thing not to be fighting with this guy anymore, but they weren't exactly friends.

"Well, uh, see you," Jason said, turning and heading for an empty table.

As Jason sat down by himself, Lee began to wonder if he should have invited Jason to sit with him. Then a bunch of other football players appeared and sat with Jason. At the same time, Michael and Jeremy walked over carrying their lunch trays.

Michael, tall and muscular, towered over Jeremy. Michael's hair was straight and blond. Freckle-faced Jeremy's hair was red, and bristly, and he wore round, wire-rimmed glasses. They didn't look at all alike. Seeing them together like this made Lee feel better that he was adopted. Michael and Jeremy looked just as different from each other as Lee looked from both of them.

"Tell me I was seeing an optical illusion," Jeremy said as he thumped down his overloaded plastic tray. He'd bought his usual lunch of cheeseburger, a double order of fries, and two containers of chocolate milk. "Tell me that wasn't Jason Whittaker standing here a minute ago."

"It was," Lee said.

Michael unloaded his grape juice, and macaroni and cheese. "He wasn't trying to pick another fight, was he?" he asked.

Lee shook his head. "He just asked me a couple of questions about the karate demonstration."

"I wouldn't trust him if I were you," hotheaded Jeremy warned. "Maybe he's trying to learn karate by talking to you, so he can use it against you in another fight."

Lee rolled his eyes. "That's ridiculous. Forget about it, OK? The fight's over."

"Not at science fair, it's not," Jeremy muttered. "I'm up against Suzanne. It's still us versus them."

"Well, don't take it out on Jason," Lee said.

Jeremy shook his container of chocolate milk so hard Lee was amazed it didn't go flying. Then he ripped open the top of the container and stabbed his plastic straw in. "It may be easy for *you* to make up with Jason," Jeremy said. "You beat him But thanks to him, it still hurts when I chew." Jeremy rubbed his lip where Jason had punched him.

"The way I heard it," Michael said, "you attacked him first."

"It doesn't matter, anyway," Jeremy said. "No one's ever going to beat me up again. When I'm a brown belt like Lee, *nobody* will mess with me."

"Worry about being a green belt first," Michael said. "You won't be able to move up until you get Pinan Shodan right."

Jeremy bristled. "What's that supposed to mean?"

"Nothing," Michael said. "I'm just stating a fact."

Lee thought back to the way Jeremy had performed the kata last night. It had a lot of rough edges. It still needed a lot of work, but at least Jeremy had the basic moves down. He just had to pay more attention while he was doing the kata so he didn't forget what he was doing.

"The kata's going to be fine," Lee said peaceably. "We just need to get in more practice, that's all."

"I know," Jeremy said. "That's why this afternoon's going to be great. I have all the stuff I need for my project, so I can spend the whole afternoon doing bunkai with you, after karate class. We can do it five

hundred times, if you want. It will be like three practice sessions in one."

"I'll settle for just one," Michael said, taking a long
swig of grape juice.

"Yo-i!" Lee signalled Jeremy a few hours later,
after karate class had ended.

Jeremy took the ready position for Pinan Shodan.
He was more than physically ready. He was mentally
ready. He wasn't going to let himself get distracted
again by thoughts of his science project. He had to
prove to his brothers, and especially to Dwight, that
he was taking this seriously. He was going to give this
bunkai his all, no matter how many times they wanted
to do it. After all, he didn't want to look like a jerk
on television.

"Hajime!" Lee commanded Jeremy to begin.

Jeremy dropped low into cat stance, blocked Michael's chest punch, and countered. Then he whipped
around and blocked Lee's attack. Almost instanta-
neously, he turned again and fought off Dwight with
a chest block and kick, then swiveled around one
hundred eighty degrees to block Michael's punches
with knife hands.

"Slow down Jeremy," Lee directed. "It looks good,
but save your energy. It's hot in here."

It *was* hot inside the dojo. The air was stuffy and stale from a class of people kicking and punching and sweating. The mirrors were all fogged up as if someone had taken a shower in there. But that didn't slow Jeremy down one little bit.

"Hyaaaaah!" Jeremy's kiai rang sharp and loud through the muggy air as he grabbed hold of Michael with his left arm and ran a spear hand through Michael's body. Actually, he ran a spear hand *next to* Michael's body, but the point was to imagine that the hand was going through.

The next move was the trickiest one. It was a three-quarter backward turn, ending in cat stance with knife hands blocking. If you did it fast enough, the momentum of your body could knock your opponent off balance. Jeremy crossed his left foot behind his right. The he spun around so fast *he* almost fell over as his arms blocked Lee's chest punch.

Jeremy didn't stop there. He blocked another punch of Lee's, then whirled to block Dwight. He was moving so fast, he was starting to feel a little dizzy.

Keep going! a voice in his head urged him. His gi felt clammy and heavy against his body, slowing him down. But Jeremy wasn't going to let anything stop him today.

Jeremy blocked, dropped low, then sprang up in a

kick to Dwight's solar plexus. He dropped low again, and repeated the sequence on the other side. Then he dropped into a low, forward-leaning stance and blocked Michael's low squatting punch to the ribs.

Jeremy was starting to see tiny black specks in the air in front of him, and his legs felt rubbery. His ears were ringing, too. But he was so close to the end. Just a few more down blocks and high blocks to go and he'd be done.

The black specks were getting larger, filling in the spaces. Jeremy forced himself to do another tricky back turn, crossing his arms in front of his body to do a low block against Lee's kick. The ringing was getting louder, and the black spots had grown and spread out so much, Jeremy could hardly see.

Just a few more moves, the voice in his head whispered, but Jeremy couldn't hear it over the ringing in his ears. His legs felt funny, too, like they weren't his anymore. He couldn't feel them at all, and he couldn't see. Suddenly he felt a pair of strong hands lifting him up. Then Jeremy felt himself being lowered gently to the floor, his back against the wall. Then he felt something cold and wet being pressed against his forehead.

As the black spots began to shrink again, Jeremy became aware of Sensei kneeling on the floor in front of him. Sensei's dark brown eyes looked worried. Lee, Michael, and Dwight stood behind him. They looked worried, too.

"Here," Sensei said, handing Jeremy a paper cup filled with water. "You're overheated. Drink this."

Jeremy drank, then he blinked a couple of times, trying to clear his vision. "What happened?" he asked.

"You almost passed out," Sensei said.

The black spots had shrunk to specks, and the ringing in Jeremy's ears had stopped. Now that he could think straight again, Jeremy began to panic. He hadn't even gotten through one complete kata. They had a lot more practice to do if they were going to be ready for the demonstration.

"I feel fine now," Jeremy said, starting to stand up.

Sensei let a heavy hand fall down on Jeremy's shoulder. "Not so fast," he said. He turned to look at the small group of people who'd gathered behind him. "Go back to what you were doing," he said.

In less than a second, everyone had scattered to other parts of the room.

"So how's Pinan Shodan bunkai going?" Sensei asked Jeremy. "It looks like you were running through the moves pretty quickly."

"Well, yes," Jeremy admitted, "but that's because

I already know what I'm doing. I'm working on speed and power now."

"Oh," Sensei said, with a faint smile. "So you already know Pinan Shodan. That's very fast for someone who just got his green belt."

Jeremy broke into a huge grin. Sensei had given him a compliment! That was practically unheard of! Sensei was saying Jeremy was a fast learner.

"Well, I had to learn fast," Jeremy said modestly. "See, I've got science fair coming up the day before the demonstration, and the only way I could get everything done was to work faster than your average person."

"And when you work this fast, what does that mean?" Sensei asked. "That you only have to do half as many kata?"

Jeremy thought hard. He hadn't calculated how much time he could save by being smarter than everybody else. "It's not really a question of how many kata," he said, "but just learning how to spend my time."

Sensei rose to his feet. "I see."

Jeremy tried to get up, too, but Sensei turned his hand palm down. "Stay there," he said. "You've overexerted yourself. After you've rested a few more minutes, I want you to shower and go home."

"But Sensei . . . " Jeremy started to say.

Sensei shook his head and walked away. Jeremy knew he shouldn't even have questioned Sensei's directions. But how could he just sit here when his brothers and Dwight were waiting to practice bunkai again? Jeremy couldn't let them waste another practice session because of him. On the other hand, he couldn't disobey Sensei. That would be the worst form of disrespect.

"It's OK," Lee said, reappearing when Sensei had crossed to the other side of the room. "We can practice tomorrow. We don't want you blacking out again."

"Yeah," Michael said. "Don't worry about it."

Jeremy didn't know which made him feel worse. His guilt that his brothers were being so understanding, or his fear that he wouldn't have time to practice with them tomorrow. Well, he'd just have to make time, that's all.

Dwight grinned down at Jeremy. "You're a madman!" he said approvingly. "The way you were blocking and kicking out there, I was just glad it wasn't a real fight. You could have killed me!"

Jeremy wasn't sure if this was good or bad. "I could try to slow it down a little when your father puts us on TV," he said, hoping Dwight wouldn't laugh in his face for assuming he'd be on the news at all.

"Are you kidding?" Dwight asked. "The more it looks like a real fight, the better it will look on television. Keep it up!"

Jeremy smiled in relief. Just a few minutes ago, he thought he'd lost it completely. Now it looked like Sensei, Dwight, and soon the whole world would see just how great he really was.

Chapter Six

Yeah, real great, Jeremy said to himself eight hours later, waving his mother's blow dryer in the air. He'd been working all night and, so far, he didn't have much to show for himself. Just ten slightly lumpy balls of newspaper strips and flour paste, spread out on the floor. Jeremy had been hoping to paint them tonight, too, but they were still soggy. He waved the blow dryer faster, hoping that would help them dry faster.

Maybe if he got the old fan out of the attic, he could set it up to blow on the row of planets. Then he'd have his hands free to work on his gear system. The only problem was, if he left his room, his parents would be sure to hear him. Then they'd know he was up two hours past his bedtime. He didn't want to get caught.

Jeremy had planned the evening very carefully.

He'd rushed through his homework after dinner so he could give his project a lot of time. At ten o'clock, he'd turned out his lights and pretended to go to sleep, waiting until he heard his parents go up to their room and close their door. Jeremy knew they always fell asleep pretty quickly. After waiting half an hour, Jeremy had turned on his desk light and gone back to work on his project.

He was nervous enough about using the blow dryer, but his parents slept at the other end of the house. Jeremy also had it set on low, and he'd stuffed a towel in the crack under his door to muffle the noise even more. They might hear him, though, if he went up to the attic. The attic was right over their bedroom.

Tap. Tap. Tap.

Jeremy turned off the blow dryer and froze. What was that sound? Was someone knocking? Had his parents found him out? Jeremy yanked the cord out of the wall, and tossed the blow dryer under his bed. He quickly turned off his light and jumped into bed.

"Jeremy!" came a loud whisper.

Jeremy sat up in the dark. That wasn't his parents calling. It was Michael. Jeremy threw off the covers, and padded across the room. He opened the door a crack. Michael and Lee were standing in the hallway in their pajamas.

63

Jeremy rubbed his eyes with his fists. "What do you want?" he asked, pretending he'd just woken up. "I'm trying to sleep."

"Yeah, right," Michael said, pushing the door open. Michael and Lee barged right past Jeremy and Michael snapped on the desk light.

"Ah-ha," he said, examining the ten wet gray balls of newspaper. Then he noticed the yellow plastic blow dryer cord sticking out from under Jeremy's bed. "So that's what we heard. You're lucky mom and dad didn't hear you."

Jeremy sat down on his bed. "Excuse me, Sherlock Holmes," he said sarcastically. "You're not going to turn me in, are you?"

Michael made a face. "Yeah right," he said. "Would I fink on my own brother? We just wanted to see what you were up to."

"Yeah," Lee said, kneeling down to look at the papier mache. "Is this your project?"

Jeremy jumped up and stood over his planets protectively. "I know it doesn't look like much, yet," he said, "but wait till they're painted. And wait till you see the gear system I've designed. It's revolutionary." Then Jeremy laughed. He'd just made a joke without realizing it. "Revolutionary!" he said. "Get it? Like planets revolving around the sun?"

Lee smiled. "Ha ha."

Michael studied the sketches Jeremy had tacked up on the bulletin board above his desk. "Looks pretty complicated," he said. "You must have a lot of work ahead of you."

Lee stood up and looked over Michael's shoulders. "Yeah," he said. "Putting all those gears together's going to take a lot of time."

"Most of it's done already," Jeremy lied, not wanting them to think his project would take him away from their bunkai. Besides, it wasn't a total lie. Most of it would be done soon. And the project *wouldn't* take him away from their bunkai because Jeremy was planning to work on it late at night. That way he could practice bunkai every afternoon, and squeeze his homework in between.

"So where is it?" Lee asked.

Jeremy was confused. "Where's what?"

"The rest of it. I want to see the gear system."

"Oh," Jeremy said, trying to figure a way out of his lie. "I can't show anybody until it's finished. But I promise you'll be the first."

Michael crossed the room and opened the door a crack. He peeked out to make sure the coast was clear. "Don't stay up too late, OK?" he said. "You don't want to be a complete burnout tomorrow."

"I'll be fine," Jeremy said confidently.

"Try to get a good night's sleep," Lee advised as he followed Michael to the door. "My balance is always off in karate when I don't get enough sleep."

Jeremy was barely listening. He was already plugging in the blow dryer so he could finish drying his papier mache planets.

Jeremy couldn't stop yawning as he sat at his desk in class the next morning. He wasn't sure what time he'd finally fallen asleep last night. He did know it was near daylight, though. He'd seen the light glowing around his pulled-down windowshades.

It had been worth it, though. He'd not only painted his planets, he'd started putting his gears together. It was cooler out today, too, which meant he could practice bunkai without getting overheated like he had yesterday. Once again, his life was under control.

Rrrrrrrrring!

The bell announced the beginning of class.

Mr. Unruh, Jeremy's math teacher, stood up behind his desk. Lean and wiry from all the marathons he ran, Mr. Unruh always wore running shoes with his suit and tie.

"Put away your books," Mr. Unruh said. "It's that time again." He tipped down his tinted aviator glasses and wiggled his eyebrows.

At first, Jeremy's cottony brain didn't register what Mr. Unruh was saying. Then he felt goosebumps and a slow sinking feeling in the pit of his stomach. Mr. Unruh was hitting them with a surprise quiz.

Ordinarily, Jeremy didn't mind when this happened. It gave him a chance to rack up a few more good scores to beef up his already pretty impressive math grade. Today, though, was not a good day. Jeremy had blitzed through his math homework last night like a speed-racer. Come to think of it, Jeremy couldn't even remember what last night's assignment *was*.

"Pass these back," Mr. Unruh told the first person in every row as he handed out stacks of papers.

Jeremy, at the back of his row, looked up to get his copy of the quiz. Kevin Whittaker, who sat a couple seats ahead of him, turned around to pass the papers back. Short and beefy, Kevin looked like a miniature version of his older brother Jason, with the same curly brown hair and green eyes. As he caught Jeremy's eye, he rolled his eyes. Kevin wasn't as good at math as Jeremy.

Jeremy shrugged back at him. After all, when you were as great as Jeremy, you didn't have to brag. It was so obvious he could afford to be modest.

When the quiz finally reached Jeremy, he quickly scanned the questions. They were all multiplying and dividing fractions. That wasn't so hard. What had he been so worried about? He'd been working hard all year. He could afford to coast for a week or two.

Jeremy uncapped his pen and quickly worked his way through the ten equations. If he hadn't been so tired, he might have been even quicker, but it didn't matter because Mr. Unruh didn't give any points for speed.

"Pencils down," Mr. Unruh said after fifteen minutes. "Hand your papers forward."

Jeremy tossed his paper over the shoulder of the guy sitting in front of him. Then he leaned back in his chair and relaxed. Kevin turned around and gave Jeremy a sad smile. He probably felt bad when he saw the real answers on Jeremy's quiz. Kevin was lucky if he scored seventy on a pop quiz.

"Now open your textbooks," Mr. Unruh directed.

Jeremy only half-listened as Mr. Unruh reviewed a lot of stuff he already knew. He'd come up with a new idea for his science project. He'd been planning to use metal rods to hang the planets from and wrap the electrical wiring around them. But what if he used hollow copper tubes? Then he could run the wires through the tubes. The whole thing would look a lot neater, and a lot more professional.

Rrrrrrring!

Class was over. Jeremy slammed his textbook shut and got up to leave. As he headed out into the hallway, Kevin Whittaker tapped him on the shoulder.

"Seventy-one eighty-firsts?" Kevin asked.

Jeremy was still thinking about copper pipes. "What?"

"Your answer for number five. I got one third. You got seventy-one eighty-firsts."

Jeremy stopped short, his sneakers squeaking against the linoleum floor. He didn't remember question five, exactly, but he did remember getting a very odd-looking fraction. Come to think of it, it had struck him as strange when he wrote it down because Mr. Unruh usually designed the questions so that, if you did it right, the answer was pretty simple. Uh-oh, Jeremy thought. Suddenly he knew he'd gotten that one completely wrong.

"You got a weird one for number seven, too," Kevin said. "I got three fifths and you got nine thirty-fifths."

Jeremy felt his face grow hot. What right did Kevin Whittaker have looking at his quiz? That was invasion of privacy! It was just like Kevin, the little twerp.

That wasn't really what made Jeremy so angry, though. The more Jeremy thought about it, the more he realized how many answers he probably got wrong. Not because he didn't know what he was doing, but because he'd been careless. He hadn't read the questions carefully. He hadn't double-checked his answers either.

But even *that* wasn't the worst part. The worst part was that dumb Kevin Whittaker had gotten the answers right while Jeremy got them wrong. That was like turning the world upside down. Jeremy was the one who was good in math. Kevin was the one who flunked most of the time.

Jeremy looked up to find Kevin Whittaker still staring at him. "What are you looking at?" he said rudely.

Kevin blinked. It wasn't all that long ago that there was a feud between the Whittakers and the Jenkinses. Now Kevin was trying to be nice, and it seemed like Jeremy was picking a fight. All of Kevin's old anger flooded back.

"I guess I'm looking at your basic jerk," he sneered back.

"Oh yeah?" Jeremy's face got even redder.

"Yeah," Kevin said hotly. "You're just mad 'cause I did better on the math quiz than you. You're acting like a big baby!"

Jeremy shoved past Kevin angrily, his fingers itching to punch Kevin's big fat head. "Bug off, Whittaker!" he yelled. He headed off down the hall at a fast and furious pace.

Kevin kept right up with him. "I'm not the only Whittaker who's going to outsmart you," he jeered.

Jeremy had to stop at his locker to get his social studies book, which only made it harder to shake Kevin. "Don't you have somewhere to go?" Jeremy asked irritably.

"Yeah," Kevin said, leaning one hand against the locker next to Jeremy's. "I'm going to the science fair to watch my sister win first prize."

I won't listen to him, Jeremy told himself as he stuffed his math textbook and notebook onto the top shelf of his locker. He couldn't let Kevin see that he'd struck a nerve. Not that Jeremy actually thought Suzanne could beat him at the fair. But Kevin wouldn't have said that unless he knew what Suzanne's project was.

Jeremy was dying to know what Suzanne was working on. It was more than just curiosity. Jeremy wanted to make himself feel better. If only he could be sure

71

Suzanne's idea really was bogus, he could relax a little more. Maybe he wouldn't feel so threatened once he knew how "fabulous" her project *wasn't*.

"Suzanne's idea is so *great*," Kevin taunted. "I'm sure it's much better than yours."

"What do you know about great ideas?" Jeremy muttered as he fished through the bottom of his locker looking for his social studies book.

"More than you," Kevin said. "I bet you'd like to know what it is, huh?"

Suddenly, Jeremy had a brilliant idea. A way to get the information out of Kevin without Kevin even realizing Jeremy cared. "It sounds more like *you're* the one who wants to tell," Jeremy said in an offhand voice. "Don't let me stop you."

Kevin snickered. "You wish, Jenkins. You're not getting any information out of me. But let me just give you one word of advice. Pull out of the science fair now, and spare yourself the humiliation of losing!"

Chapter Seven

"The bunkai's looking really good," Lee told Jeremy the following Wednesday. The three brothers were coasting their bicycles into the garage. They were coming home from karate, where they'd spent an hour after class practicing for the demonstration.

"Your form's improved a lot," Michael added, hopping off his black ten speed. "I think all we need now is a little more speed, and we'll be looking good on Sunday."

Speed! thought Jeremy with a grimace as he dropped heavily off his bike. All those late nights putting his model together were beginning to slow him down. He had this unreal sensation all the time, like he was moving underwater. But it would be over soon. His science project was more than halfway finished, and he could do Pinan Shodan backwards and forwards.

Lee sniffed the air as he opened the door in the garage that opened into the house. "Mmmm," he said. "Smells like dad's already started dinner."

Jeremy's mouth began to water as he headed down the hall to the kitchen. It smelled like ginger and garlic and peppers. He felt less tired already.

"Hi, guys," Mr. Jenkins said as they entered. Tall and well built, he wore jeans and a T-shirt that said No Nukes. Jeremy's dad used to be an officer in the army, but now he ran the local recycling center, and he was really into saving the environment. He stood by the stove, stir-frying vegetables in a wok. "Ready to man your stations?" he asked. That meant it was time to check the duty roster on the refrigerator to see what their pre-dinner chores were.

"Yes, sir!" Michael and Lee said, saluting crisply.

Jeremy hesitated. He didn't want to wimp out of his job, but he still had a lot of work left to do on his science project, and the fair was only three days away. Maybe if he did his chore really fast, he'd still have time left before dinner to do a little more work on his project.

"What's the matter, Jeremy?" his father asked as

Jeremy stood motionless in the middle of the kitchen floor.

"Hmmm?" Jeremy looked up at his father.

"You look beat," his father said. "Are you feeling okay?"

Jeremy stifled a yawn. "I'm fine, Dad." He walked over to the refrigerator and checked the duty roster. He was on salad tonight. Jeremy opened the refrigerator and pulled out a head of lettuce.

"I guess you've been working pretty hard, huh?" Mr. Jenkins asked, throwing some marinated strips of chicken into the wok with the vegetables. They started sizzling as soon as they hit the hot metal.

"*Very* hard," Lee said proudly. "You should see his Pinan Shodan."

"All I see are dark circles under his eyes," Mr. Jenkins said worriedly. "Maybe you should take a little nap before dinner, Jeremy."

Jeremy paused, the head of lettuce still in his hand. "But who's going to make the salad?" he asked.

"I'll do it," Michael volunteered. "You deserve a break. But don't think I'm *always* going to be this nice." Michael took the lettuce out of Jeremy's hand.

"I don't know if I could sleep," Jeremy protested weakly.

"So rest, then," his father told him.

"Well, if you're sure you don't mind . . ."

"Go, already!" Michael said firmly.

Gratefully, Jeremy trudged up the stairs to his room. Come to think of it, a nap wasn't such a bad idea. Then he'd have more energy to work later. Jeremy stumbled into his room, and fell diagonally across his bed. He fell instantly asleep, his sneakered feet hanging, toes down, over the edge of the mattress.

At last.

Jeremy's model of the solar system was finally finished. Jeremy could hardly believe it. He could hardly keep his eyes open, either. After his nap and stir-fried chicken, Jeremy had worked on his model straight into the night. The clock said one A.M., but Jeremy didn't care. The important thing was that his model was beautiful.

The sun, now painted a metallic gold, had a hollow copper tube running through its center. The copper tube was mounted on a circular base which supported the whole contraption. The top of the tube ran up through the sun into a central gear shaft. Nine hollow copper rods of varying lengths radiated from the gear shaft. Each rod had a papier mache planet hanging from the end of it and a tiny gear to control the planet's rotation. A wire running down through the base attached to a small box with an on-off switch and a speed control lever.

"Brilliant!" Jeremy whispered, staring at his creation by the light of his desk lamp. All he had to do now was make sure it worked.

Before Jeremy could flip the switch, he heard footsteps in the hallway. It was probably Michael and Lee again, but just in case it wasn't, Jeremy started to tiptoe towards his bed. Maybe whoever it was would just think he fell asleep with the light on. Oops! Too late. The door flew open before Jeremy could get in and pull the covers up.

"Jeremy!" His parents stood in the doorway in their bathrobes.

Jeremy blinked and smiled guiltily. "Hi," he said lamely. "I guess you're wondering what I'm doing up so late."

Jeremy's parents went over by the model of the solar system, surveying it. "We know exactly what you've been doing every night," Jeremy's mom said, lightly touching the copper rod Saturn hung from. "By the way, I'd like my blow dryer back, if you're done with it."

Jeremy stared, flabbergasted, at his parents. "You mean you've known all along?"

Mr. Jenkins turned to Jeremy with an amused expression on his face. "We're down the hall, not across the street," he said. "You didn't think you were pulling one over on us, did you?"

Jeremy sank down onto his bed. "I can't believe this!" he said. "How come you didn't say anything to me about staying up so late? How come I didn't get in trouble?"

"You've got a lot on your plate right now," his father said. "We know you needed the extra time. We didn't want to hassle you."

"But we also want you to be able to get up for school tomorrow," his mother said pointedly.

"I will, I promise," he said. "Anyway, my model's finished, see? I was just going to get in bed, honest!"

"Looks pretty good," Mr. Jenkins said, walking all the way around the model. "Does it work?"

"I don't know yet," Jeremy admitted. "I haven't turned it on."

"Can we see?" his mother asked.

Jeremy wasn't sure how to answer. He was just as eager to show his parents the model in motion as they were to see it. But he wanted to make sure everything was perfect first. "I want to check a few things over before that," Jeremy said. "Maybe tomorrow?"

"No problem," Mr. Jenkins said. "You let us know when you're ready."

Mrs. Jenkins looked disappointed, but she didn't object. "Just promise you'll go to sleep *soon*," she said, kissing Jeremy's cheek.

"A couple more minutes, and I'll be out like a light," Jeremy said.

Mr. Jenkins ruffled Jeremy's hair. "G'night."

As his parents left the room, Jeremy felt a lump rise in his throat. They had to be the greatest parents in the world for letting him break the rules and being so understanding about it. Jeremy's brothers were pretty great, too, for taking over his chores just so he would have more time to get everything done.

Jeremy was going to pay them back, though. Every one of them. When he won first prize at the science fair and they called him up to the podium to accept his trophy and five-thousand-dollar scholarship, he was going to tell everyone in the audience that he couldn't have done it without the support of his family.

Then, after he got discovered at the karate demonstration and became a big star in martial arts movies, he'd use his fame and glory to help them all. When Jeremy got interviewed on talk shows, he'd give a free plug to Turbotron, so his mother would be able to sell more comic books, and he'd tell everyone to recycle since his father ran a recycling plant. Maybe he could even get Lee and Michael parts in his movies.

Of course, being a movie star wouldn't stop Jeremy from being a straight A student. And after he retired from the movies, he'd still have time to be a famous scientist. Maybe even an astronomer or astronaut.

To think it all started here, in this narrow room, with the flick of a switch. Jeremy picked up the control box for his model and placed his finger on the on-off switch. This was the moment that would change the rest of his life. Suddenly, Jeremy wasn't tired anymore but electrified. With his eyes glued to the model, Jeremy flicked the switch.

Nothing happened. At first. Then, slowly, the planets began to move around the sun and spin on their axes.

"Come on," Jeremy coaxed, pushing up the speed control lever. "You can go faster than that."

The planets seemed to answer Jeremy, picking up speed. But the most wonderful part was, each one was revolving around the sun and rotating on its axis in direct proportion to the actual planets. Mars took almost twice as long to get around the sun as Earth, but it rotated at almost the same speed. Jupiter took more than ten times as long to get around the sun as Earth, but it rotated three times as fast.

The planets slowed down again even though Jeremy hadn't touched the lever. OK, so it wasn't perfect yet, but it was pretty close. Jeremy made a mental note to check the wiring on the speed control when he got a chance. But now he could hardly wait for tomorrow to show his parents and his brothers what he'd made. They'd all be so proud of him. And they'd be right.

Chapter Eight

Clink! Clink, clink! Lee's sai clanged against the sai of Rosalie Davis, Sensei's daughter, as the two of them dueled in the dojo. It was five thirty on Friday afternoon. They were warming up for the final rehearsal before Sunday's karate demonstration. Jeremy stood nearby, watching.

Rosalie, several inches taller than Lee and much thicker, was the attacker. Her light brown ponytail flippd up and down as she lunged at Lee with her short metal sword. Lee was smaller, but he was quick and skillful. He easily parried Rosalie's strikes.

The fight with such sharp and deadly weapons looked dangerous. Jeremy knew it wasn't. Both Lee and Rosalie were in perfect control. Neither one of them would get hurt.

Jeremy couldn't help feeling a little jealous. Lee

and Rosalie were going to attract a lot of attention at the demonstration. Weapons were so much flashier than plain kata. But, Jeremy reminded himself, *his* bunkai demonstration would be just as good because he was one person fighting against three attackers. That had to impress people. And Jeremy had one thing in his bunkai that Lee and Rosalie didn't have— Dwight Vernon. Dwight's father, Vic Vernon, wasn't going to ignore his own son when he videotaped his segment for the WMID-TV news.

Jeremy looked around the dojo at the other students warming up. Groups of white belts, green belts, brown belts, and black belts, adults and kids, practiced together or did stretching exercises on the mat. There had to be at least fifty people altogether.

Six brown belts stood in a straight line at attention. Sempai Seeger, a tall second-degree black belt with shaggy hair, stood nearby. *Sempai* meant "senior student" in Japanese. You were supposed to address any student who had higher rank than you as sempai. Technically, Lee and Michael were sempai to Jeremy. On the other hand, Jeremy was sempai to all the white belts, even the ones who were grown-ups.

"Kata!" shouted Sempai Seeger.

"Kata!" answered the brown belts.

"*Naihanchi Sho!*" Sempai Seeger shouted.

"Naihanchi Sho!" they answered.

The white belt katas were called the Fukyugata, or basic, katas. The green belt katas were called Pinan, or intermediate, katas. The Naihanchi, or brown belt, katas were even more advanced. Most of the katas moved in eight different directions, but Naihanchi Sho, the first brown belt kata, only moved sideways, to the right or left. This was supposed to simulate a fight where a person was backed up against a wall.

At Sempai Seeger's command, the brown belts began their moves, stomping heavily on the shiny wooden floor. After each move, they'd pause, and Sempai Seeger would walk back and forth in front of the line. Then Sempai Seeger would do something unexpected, like pounding on their arms with his fists, or kicking their legs, trying to make them fall over. Sometimes he'd even jump on their backs to see if they could hold their stance.

This was called body testing, and it was only done on brown belts and higher ranks. The purpose was to toughen students, get them used to withstanding attacks, and to make sure they always had secure footing. Jeremy couldn't wait until he was old enough to be tested. He was sure no one would be able to knock him down.

That reminded him. He should probably be practicing with Michael and Dwight and the green belt group practicing *Pinan Nidan*, the second green belt kata. Jeremy didn't want them to think he was goofing off, but he was trying to save his energy for the rehearsal.

Jeremy had gone to bed early last night, but it didn't make up for all the nights he'd stayed up late the past two weeks. He couldn't stop yawning, and all day he'd felt like he wanted to lie down wherever he was and close his eyes for a few minutes.

Still, he'd made it this far. He'd make it the rest of the way, too. The science fair was tomorrow, and Jeremy was ready. Aside from a little speed control problem Jeremy planned to fix tonight, his solar system was working perfectly. Jeremy was sure his Pinan Shodan bunkai would go just as well. Maybe he hadn't put in quite as much time on either project as he would have liked, but that was the price you paid for being multi-talented. You had to spread yourself a little thin sometimes.

Jeremy glanced up at Sensei's bulletin board, and scanned the index cards thumbtacked to it. Sensei was always putting up new quotes for his students to think about. Jeremy had read most of them, but a new one caught his eye:

The less effort, the faster and more powerful you will be.

—Bruce Lee

It had to be fate, Jeremy thought as he reread the words on the index card. That quote was all about him! Maybe Sensei had even put it up on the board after he complimented Jeremy on how fast he'd learned Pinan Shodan. Maybe Sensei was saying that Jeremy was so smart that he didn't have to try as hard as other people. Jeremy was able to accomplish more with less effort.

"Shotu-mate," Sempai Seeger shouted in Japanese, ordering everyone to stop whatever they were doing.

Lee and Rosalie stopped dueling, and everyone else leaped to attention as Sensei Davis entered the deck from his office.

"*Sensei ni mawate*," barked Sempai Seeger.

Still standing at attention, everyone turned in the direction of Sensei Davis.

"Sensei ni rei!" Sempai Seeger commanded.

Everyone bowed to Sensei and shouted "*Onegai-shimasu*, Sensei!" This was Japanese for *please teach me*.

"Onegai-shimasu," Sensei said back to them. In

karate, Jeremy had learned, anyone could learn from anyone, no matter what their rank.

"We'll have a quick warm-up," Sensei Davis directed them. "Then, instead of a regular class, we'll have a run-through of our program for Sunday. Shugo! Line up!"

The wooden floor thumped as all the colored belts and white belts sorted themselves out. Within seconds, they had formed two long straight lines that stretched from the front of the dojo, all the way to the back. Jeremy stood at attention behind a green-belt woman with frizzy hair.

"Seiza, sit," Sensei said in a quiet voice.

Everyone sat on the deck, their legs folded beneath them. Then they closed their eyes and rested their palms, face up, on the knots of their belts.

With his eyes closed, Jeremy found it even harder to stay awake. The dojo was so quiet and still, even with lots of other people all around him. He could barely even hear anyone else breathing. If only he could stay like that for a few hours, just until he caught up on his sleep.

The crack of Sensei's hands clapping together jolted Jeremy's eyes open. After bowing to Sensei, everyone stood up and went through five minutes of knee bends, stretches, neck rolls, side bends, and light jumping up and down. Then Sensei clapped his hands again, and everyone stood still.

"We'll have everyone sitting on the matted deck, facing the back of the dojo," Sensei said. "Sempai Seeger, Sempai Brooks, please join me in the back."

"Arigato, Sensei!" the students shouted as two black belts followed Sensei Davis to the wooden deck. Sempai Brooks was a balding man with a beard and mustache. Like Sempai Seeger, he was a second-degree black belt. They both taught some of the adult classes.

Jeremy found a spot on the mat and sat, crosslegged, between Lee and Michael. While Sensei Davis picked up his clipboard from a bench at the back of the room, the two black belts unfolded some metal folding chairs. Then Sensei and the two black belts sat down.

"When I call your name, please take your place on the wooden deck in front of me," Sensei Davis said. "Sempai Brooks, you'll observe, please, and make corrections."

"Arigato, Sensei!" said Sempai Brooks, crossing his arms over his stomach.

"White belts!" Sensei called. "Adults and children. On the spot for Fukyugata Ichi, first kata."

Eight white belt students, including Kevin Whittaker, raced up to the wooden deck and formed two lines in front of Sensei.

"Onegai-shimasu, Sensei!" they cried together, bowing.

"Onegai-shimasu," Sensei answered. "By the count. Sempai Brooks counting. Yo-i!"

The white belts crossed their palms in front of themselves as they assumed the ready position.

"*Ichi!*" Sempai Brooks counted the number one in Japanese.

The white belts turned left into a down block, lunging forward on a bent left leg while striking downward with their left arms.

"*Ni!*" Sempai Brooks counted two.

The white belts stepped forward on the right foot and punched with their right hands.

Sempai Brooks stopped counting. He walked around the white belts, studying them carefully. Then he paused in front of Kevin Whittaker.

"Straighten out that wrist," Sempai Brooks said, pushing down the top of Kevin's fist, which was bent back so the knuckles pointed straight up. It was important when punching to keep the wrist absolutely straight to deliver the full power of the body.

Kevin looked embarrassed as he shouted "Arigato,

Sempai!" Jeremy couldn't help smiling. Kevin deserved it for making fun of Jeremy's answers on the math quiz. Now it was his turn.

The white belts finished their kata. "Arigato, Sensei!" they shouted.

"Arigato," Sensei said. "Next up, Jeremy Jenkins, Michael Jenkins, Lee Jenkins, Dwight Vernon."

Lee and Michael jumped from their sitting positions right up to the soles of their feet. Jeremy tried to do the same, but his legs had fallen asleep, just like the rest of him wanted to. Jeremy rose clumsily, and slapped his feet sharply against the wood, trying to wake them up.

"A little less of the elephant idea," Sensei said as Jeremy clomped noisily to his place. "We don't want to telegraph to the enemy that we're here."

A few kids snickered, and Jeremy felt his face grow hot. He hadn't meant to sound like a wild herd in the jungle. "Arigato!" he shouted. This wasn't the glorious opening he'd pictured in his mind. But he still had a chance to make up for it.

"No count," Sensei told them. "Yo-i."

Jeremy took a shoulders-width stance and held clenched fists down in front of him. On either side of him and behind him, his brothers and Dwight raised their fists to their chest, preparing to attack him.

"Hajime!" Sensei told them to begin.

Jeremy couldn't afford to mess up now. He wasn't going to lose his focus or go too fast or make any of the mistakes he'd made before. He was going to do each move perfectly. Jeremy dropped low and pivoted to the left in cat stance, blocking with both arms as Michael threw a punch at his face. Jeremy made sure his weight was almost all on the bent back leg. He made sure his right arm, which was blocking high, had a perfectly straight wrist.

Jeremy was thinking so hard about technique that he almost didn't react when Michael threw a follow-up punch to his solar plexus. It took him a little longer than he wanted, too, to swivel around and block Lee's punch. Jeremy wasn't worried, though. The important thing was that he managed to get through the rest of the kata without any mistakes. His timing would be better after he'd gotten a good night's sleep. So far, so good. Their bunkai went off without a hitch.

"Arigato, Sensei!" they all shouted when they were finished.

"Arigato," Sensei said as the four boys backed away from him. Proper courtesy meant you could never turn your back on a black belt.

"How was it?" Jeremy whispered to Michael as they sat down on the mat.

"It was a little slow," Michael said. "We'll need to do it faster than that."

"Of course we will!" Jeremy hissed. "I'm just a little tired. I'll be fine on Sunday."

"No talking!" Sempai Brooks snapped, turning a fierce eye on Jeremy.

Why was everyone being so critical of him today? First they told him he walked like an elephant, then they said he was too slow, now they were saying he was too loud. Jeremy felt so angry he wanted to jump to his feet and do his kata all over again, just to show them all how wrong they were. But he'd have his chance on Sunday. Once he was up in front of that audience and those TV cameras, he'd have so much energy, his brothers wouldn't know what hit them.

Chapter Nine

"Careful," Jeremy warned his father as they stood in the cool darkness of the garage, Saturday morning. "There's a lot of delicate gears in there."

"I know," Mr. Jenkins said as he slid Jeremy's solar system model into the back of his Jeep. "Don't worry. I've got everything under control." He smiled and patted Jeremy on the back. "Relax, OK?"

Jeremy bit his lower lip as his father carefully placed the delicate-looking project on a bed of blankets and bubble wrap. Jeremy knew he was just nervous. His father was handling the model as carefully as if it were made of eggshells. Still, it was hard to be calm when the science fair was less than an hour away.

"Dad, can we hurry up a little?" Jeremy asked, pulling up the sleeve of his sportcoat to check his watch. He hadn't wanted to wear a jacket and tie, but his mother had insisted. She said the judges wouldn't just be looking at his project, and that it was important to make a nice impression. Jeremy hated being all dressed up. He felt like a geek. He also felt like a wet washcloth.

Jeremy had gone right to bed after dinner last night. He was so tired he thought he'd fall asleep instantly, but his mind was too full of buzzing thoughts to let him even close his eyes. He'd rehearsed his speech for the science fair judges over and over, even though he already had it memorized. He'd practiced Pinan Shodan in his mind. He'd thought about what he'd say to Vic Vernon if he got interviewed on camera. And when he was done with his interview, he started in on his science fair speech again. Jeremy had tossed and turned for hours. When he finally fell asleep, he'd dreamed he was doing Pinan Shodan, so it wasn't a very restful night for him at all.

"That should do it," Mr. Jenkins said, covering the copper rods and planets with more bubble wrap and a couple of old towels. "Tell everybody we're ready to go."

Jeremy raced into the kitchen where Michael and Lee were finishing breakfast. "Come on, you guys," he rushed them. "We're going to be late!"

Michael stood up and carried his empty glass and plate to the sink. "Calm down," he said. "It's only ten minutes away."

"Where's Mom?" Jeremy asked, ignoring him. "She always takes so long to get ready. Mom!" he screamed, running to the front hall.

His mother was already coming down the stairs, clipping big gold earrings on as she ran. "I'm ready! I'm ready!" she said. She wore a red dress with gold buttons, and her coppery hair was pulled back in a neat twist.

"Whoa, Mom, you look great," Lee told her.

Mrs. Jenkins smiled as she grabbed her purse off the kitchen counter. "Well, I figure everyone's going to come up to me when it's over to congratulate me on what a brilliant son I have, so I wanted to look my best."

"He's my brilliant son, too," Mr. Jenkins said, popping his head inside the kitchen. "But if we don't get going now, he won't have enough time to set up."

"So what are we waiting for?" Mrs. Jenkins asked, pushing past her husband. She jumped into the front seat of the Jeep and slammed the door.

Jeremy climbed into the back seat, between his brothers, and his dad got in behind the wheel. After a short drive through suburban streets and a winding, tree-lined road, they pulled up behind a long line of cars at the back entrance to the county center.

The county center was a large white building with tall Roman-looking columns all the way around it. The back looked almost like the front, with broad stone steps leading up to four oversized doors. Today, the steps were filled with boys and girls and parents lugging big cardboard boxes, suitcases, and all sorts of important-looking stuff towards the back doors.

"We'll help you unload, Jeremy," Lee said as their father turned off the ignition. "You won't be able to carry all that stuff by yourself."

"Thanks," Jeremy said, scooting out of the Jeep after Michael. "Please be careful, OK? I'll have a heart attack if anything goes wrong."

Mr. Jenkins opened the back of the Jeep. Jeremy and Lee took either end of the model, still wrapped in bubble wrap, and started up the stairs. Michael followed carrying several large pieces of cardboard painted dark blue with tiny dots of yellow and white. Jeremy had decided to add this starry backdrop in a last-minute burst of inspiration. Now his solar system would look like it was floating in space. It would be awesomely authentic.

"We're going to find a place to park," Mr. Jenkins

said, climbing back inside the Jeep next to Mrs. Jenkins. "We'll come find you inside."

Jeremy and Lee carried the model gingerly between them. When they reached the top of the stairs, they passed through one of the doors into a huge lobby with a gigantic, glittering light hanging in its center. Hundreds of people were milling around, and their voices echoed against the marble walls. Jeremy tried to curve his body around his model so no one could bump into it accidentally.

"Where do we go now?" Michael asked.

Jeremy spotted Miss Wilson standing near a long table beneath a sign that read INFORMATION. As usual, she was wearing a white labcoat over her dress, and her bifocals dangled from the chain around her neck. Moving slowly through the crowd, Jeremy headed his team toward the table.

"Hi, Jeremy," Miss Wilson said, peering at the folded-up copper pipes through the bubble wrap. She smiled at Lee and Michael. "So I finally get a chance to see your project. What is it?"

"It's working model of the solar system," Jeremy told her proudly. "It spins and rotates, just like the real thing."

Miss Wilson nodded. "That's nice." She flipped

through some papers she had stapled together. "Now, let's see—you'll be in the main exhibition hall, aisle thirteen, booth four. You'll set up there for the morning. At some point the judges will come by and inspect your project. Then, in the afternoon, you'll be able to wheel your booth to the auditorium to make your formal, three-minute presentation on the main stage. I'll come by before then to let you know what time you'll be going on. Any questions?"

Yeah, Jeremy wanted to say. *How come you play favorites with Suzanne Whittaker and not me?* When Miss Wilson had seen Suzanne's blueprints, she'd raved about it. Wonderful, she'd said, so original, and very clever. So where did she get off telling Jeremy his project was just "nice?" Of course, she hadn't really been able to see the full potential of Jeremy's model. When it was all set up, she'd feel sorry she hadn't recognized genius when she saw it. But all Jeremy asked now was, "Where's the exhibition hall?"

Miss Wilson pointed to a wide marble archway behind her. "Through the double doors," she said.

Jeremy, Lee, and Michael followed Miss Wilson's directions, and found themselves standing in an enormous room with an incredibly high ceiling. Numbered signs hung from above. Beneath each sign was a long, wide aisle with booths on either side.

Jeremy spotted sign number thirteen hanging near the middle of the room. "That's us," he said, pointing. "Let's go."

"Wow!" Michael exclaimed as they made their way past glowing computer screens with moving images on them, strange-looking contraptions made of metal, and giant plastic models of molecules and atoms. "I didn't realize there would be this many people."

"It doesn't matter how many people there are," Jeremy said confidently. "The only one who matters is me. That's the only way to succeed, you know. You can't worry about the competition."

"Oh, I know that," Michael said as they turned down aisle thirteen and stopped at the empty booth with number four painted on the floor in front of it. "I was just saying."

Jeremy paused to look at the booth. It was a wooden platform, three feet by three feet, on metal wheels. Attached to the platform were three pieces of fiberboard, about five feet tall, forming a back wall and side walls.

Lee touched the booth with his foot, and it rolled slightly. "I get it," he said. "Once you set up your project inside the booth, it becomes portable."

"These walls are perfect," Jeremy said, handing the model to Lee and taking the pieces of cardboard from

Michael. "I brought some tape and thumbtacks. We can attach the star backdrop to the walls, then stand up the model in the middle."

With his brothers' help, Jeremy taped up his backdrop, then stood his model on the platform. Removing the bubble wrap, Jeremy spread out the nine metal rods so that they were ranged around the central shaft bisecting the sun. The nine planets dangled from the rods.

"Now all I need to do is turn it on," Jeremy said, picking up the control box which was connected by a wire to the metal base.

Jeremy flipped the switch and held his breath. His brothers stared at the planets, waiting.

The planets slowly started to spin, and at the same time, they began to travel around the sun with a steady, whirring sound. Seen against the starry backdrop, it was easy to imagine you were in outer space.

"Cool," Michael said.

"Very realistic," Lee added.

"It's brilliant, that's what it is," said Mrs. Jenkins. "My son the genius."

Jeremy turned and saw his parents standing behind them. His mother had a huge grin on her freckled face, and his father was nodding and smiling.

This had to be one of the best moments of Jeremy's life. Here he was with his family around him, and his model working perfectly, and everyone so proud of him. Jeremy was so happy, he could almost forget how tired he was. And in just a few more hours, he'd feel even happier and they'd be even prouder when the judges announced him as the first place winner.

"Good job, Jeremy," his father said. "Do you want us to stay here while you wait for the judges?"

"Nah," Jeremy said. "Who knows *when* they'll get here. You might as well walk around or something."

Mr. Jenkins put his arm around his wife. "OK," he said. "We'll see you a little later. Good luck."

As their parents walked away, Michael turned to Jeremy. "You know," he said, "I was thinking. You said you wanted to know what Suzanne Whittaker's project was. Now's our chance to find out."

"Yeah!" Jeremy said. "I can't go anywhere since I have to wait for the judges, but you guys could be my spies. Not that she's any competition, of course. I'm just curious."

"Miss Wilson can tell us what booth Suzanne has," Michael said. "And we'll check out everybody else, too, and report back to you."

"Good idea," Jeremy said. *Meanwhile, I'll practice my speech a couple more times,* he thought. As his brothers headed down the aisle, Jeremy pulled a folded-up piece of paper out of his pants pocket. Silently moving his lips, he began to read the lines he already knew by heart. *Ladies and gentlemen,* he said to himself, imagining himself up on stage, under the spotlight. *Come with me on a journey through the stars . . .*

The steady whirring sound began to waver and slow down. Then Jeremy heard a funny creaking sound. Looking up, he noticed the planets had slowed down again, like they had done the first night he'd tested his model. *Oh no!* Jeremy thought. The batteries were brand new. How could this have happened?

Jeremy's heart fell down to his stomach. He'd meant to check the speed control last night, but he'd been so tired after the karate rehearsal that he'd forgot. But he wasn't about to panic. There was still time to fix it. Jeremy racked his brains for a reason this could be happening. Was something wrong with the wiring? Maybe the problem was in the speed control lever? Jeremy had a mini-screwdriver attached to his Swiss Army knife. Maybe he could take the control box apart and . . .

Jeremy gasped. Three men and one woman, all

carrying clipboards and all wearing round buttons that read Judge, Dorchester County Science Fair, were heading down the aisle, right towards his booth! Of all times for his planets to slow down. This was a disaster!

The judges were only a few feet away. Frantically, Jeremy jiggled the speed control lever. *Come on, planets,* he prayed. *Don't do this to me . . .*

The whirring sound became steady again, and the planets picked up speed just as the judges stopped in front of Jeremy's booth. Jeremy tried not to let the relief show on his face as he smiled at the judges.

"Jeremy Jenkins?" one of the men asked. "Midvale Middle School?"

Jeremy nodded. The judges looked over his project and scribbled notes on printed forms attached to their clipboards. Then they walked quickly down the aisle, stopping at another booth.

Jeremy was disappointed. He'd been hoping the judges would say something or give some indication of what they thought. But they probably didn't have time with all the projects they had to look at. No matter how much they liked something, they had to keep moving so they could look at everything before the morning was over. It was only fair.

But things were going to be a lot different this afternoon. Jeremy was sure of that. Once the judges heard his presentation, they weren't going to think about anyone else or want to look at anyone else. They wouldn't have to. Because that's when they'd realize they'd already found their winner.

Chapter Ten

An hour later, Jeremy hadn't figured out what was wrong with the speed control, but the problem seemed to have fixed itself. He'd turned his model on and off at least ten times and, every time, the planets spun perfectly. Jeremy felt foolish for even worrying. Everything was going to be fine.

Jeremy spotted his brothers walking slowly up the aisle. "Hey!" Jeremy called to them. "How the fair?"

"It's OK," Michael said, without much enthusiasm.

Jeremy smiled smugly. The other exhibits must have been really boring. "Did you find Suzanne's booth?" he asked.

Lee nodded.

"And?" Jeremy prodded.

Lee shrugged. "It was good."

"Just good?" Jeremy asked. "What was it?"

"It's hard to describe," Michael said. "She sort of modified this toy truck."

"Oh-ho!" Jeremy gloated. "That doesn't sound like much of a project."

Miss Wilson appeared from the crowd that roamed up and down the aisle. "Hi, Jeremy," she said. "You ready for part two?"

"Is it time already?" Jeremy asked, checking his watch. It was ten to twelve.

"You'll be going on at twelve fifteen," Miss Wilson said, consulting her list. "Right after Suzanne Whittaker. You can start wheeling your booth to the main auditorium. The door's at the end of this aisle, and leads right backstage. After Suzanne finishes her presentation, you'll have time to set up."

"Got it," Jeremy said, his heart starting to pound at the thought of facing so many people.

"I've got to find the rest of the Midvale people," Miss Wilson said. "Good luck, Jeremy." Her tall, slim figure quickly disappeared back into the crowd.

Jeremy turned off his model and placed the control box on the platform. Then he got behind his booth and found a metal handle attached to the back of it.

"I'll be the lookout," Lee volunteered. "I can clear the aisle in front of you and make sure you don't bump into anything."

"And I'll help you push," Michael said, getting next to Jeremy.

A few minutes later, Jeremy found himself standing in the wings of the auditorium's main stage. His brothers had gone out into the auditorium to join their parents. Giant velvet curtains stretched high above Jeremy's head, disappearing into the murky blackness. Onstage, under the harsh glare of stage lights, a boy was speaking into a microphone and talking about an experiment he'd done with potted plants.

There was applause, and the curtains glided shut. The boy wheeled his booth offstage, and Suzanne Whittaker appeared next to Jeremy, pushing her booth towards center stage. Jeremy tried not to watch her as she set up for her presentation. He knew he'd be better off practicing his speech. But he couldn't help wondering what she was doing.

Suzanne took several items out of her booth—a milk carton, a book, and a pair of glasses—and set them down on the stage. Next, she picked up a strange-looking vehicle with a metal arm coming out of the top of it and set it down. Then she took a folding chair out of the booth and set it up near the front of the stage. Wheeling her now-empty booth to the back of the stage, she returned to the chair and sat down facing the audience.

Jeremy was totally perplexed. This didn't look like any science project he'd ever seen.

The curtains opened again, and Suzanne stood up. "Good afternoon, ladies and gentlemen," she said, nervously tucking her hair behind her ears. Jeremy noticed she was wearing a navy blue dress with a white lace collar and black patent leather shoes. Jeremy was sort of glad now that his mother made him dress up. After all, he didn't want to look like a slob compared to Suzanne.

Suzanne lifted the truck off the stage and held it up. "I suppose you're wondering what this is," she said, and the audience laughed good-naturedly. "Well, I can tell you what it used to be. It used to be my little brother's remote-controlled dump truck."

Jeremy snorted. Did Suzanne honestly think she had a chance of winning the science fair by showing off one of Kevin's old toys? Jeremy was angry with himself for even listening when Kevin bragged about his sister. Kevin was full of hot air, as usual.

"Now, though," Suzanne went on, putting the dump truck down, "I call it a 'Helping Hand.'" Suzanne unfolded the metal arm on top of the truck and showed what looked like a mechanical hand at the end of it, with jointed metal fingers and a thumb. "I've modified this truck to help people who can't get around easily," Suzanne said. "It's now a remote-controlled robot, equipped with an infrared eye, which can move around the house and bring things to people who can't get up and get them themselves."

Suzanne stood up and walked to the milk carton, which she picked up off the stage. "I've labeled normal household objects with bar codes, like the ones you find on products at the supermarket," she said. "The robot can identify each object by reading the code with its 'eye.' And I tell the robot which object I want by punching the code of the object into my remote control. I'll demonstrate."

Suzanne put the milk carton down and went back to sit in her chair, the robot at her feet. "Let's say I want to read a book," Suzanne told the audience. "The code I use for that is three three nine."

Suzanne pressed three numbers on her keypad. Instantly, the truck sprang to life. It turned sharply and rolled around Suzanne's chair, heading straight for the book. It stopped a foot away from the book and lowered its mechanical arm. Then the "hand" opened up and closed around the book. Lifting the book, the truck returned to Suzanne, who took the book and said "Thank you!"

There was more laughter and scattered applause. Suzanne stood up, clutching the book to her chest.

"My device is still somewhat crude," she said, "but I'm hoping to obtain a patent on it and refine it so I can help homebound people feel more independent." Suzanne gave a little bow.

As the curtains closed, the applause was so loud, Jeremy had to cover his ears with his hands. But nothing he did could shut out the realization that he'd underestimated Suzanne. Yes, she'd modified a toy for her project, but that wasn't the point. Her idea was great! And very complicated. A lot more complicated than his.

Jeremy looked at his model of the solar system and began to feel his face grow hot with embarrassment. A couple of papier mache planets couldn't possibly compare to a truck that brought you milk and cookies. The more Jeremy looked at his project, the more it was beginning to look like a simple mobile. His heart began to pound and his palms grew sticky. He could feel his sweat soaking into his hair.

"Good luck, Jeremy," Suzanne said, wheeling her booth full of equipment past him, towards the exit.

Jeremy didn't respond. He had nothing to say to her. He wasn't going to let her ruin his day, he thought, as he wheeled his booth onto the stage. He couldn't wimp out now, in front of the judges and all the people in the audience. Besides, maybe he wasn't giving his idea enough credit. It hadn't been that easy to design planets that could spin *and* travel around the sun at the same time. And picking up a book or a milk carton was so *ordinary*. That wasn't science. The solar system was science.

The curtains opened in front of Jeremy. The spotlights shining in his eyes were so bright, he could barely see the audience. There was a hanging microphone a few feet above his head.

"Ladies and gentlemen," Jeremy said, in his best circus ringmaster voice, "come with me on a journey through the stars . . ."

Jeremy moved to the side of his booth so that everyone could see his model. "Imagine yourself on a spaceship," Jeremy said, "traveling through the Milky Way towards a star 864,000 miles in diameter and with an average surface temperature of 10,000 degrees Fahrenheit. That's our sun."

Jeremy was feeling better already. All these facts and figures were bound to impress the judges. Suzanne hadn't given even one in *her* speech.

"I've built a working model of the solar system," Jeremy said proudly. "But not only do my planets rotate on their axes and revolve around the sun . . ."

Jeremy picked up his control box and pressed the "On" switch. The planets obediently began to twirl and move around the metallic gold sun. There were some murmurs from the audience.

". . . But their speed is in direct proportion to the actual speed of the actual planets!" Jeremy said triumphantly, looking out at the audience. "How have I accomplished this?" Out of the corner of his eye, Jeremy noticed that the planets seemed to be slowing down again, but maybe the audience was too far away to see this. "I've designed an elaborate system of gears . . ."

There was no escaping it. The planets were moving so slowly they'd almost stopped. Trying not to panic, Jeremy jiggled the speed control lever. To his great relief, the planets started to move faster. ". . . An elaborate system of gears," Jeremy continued, "which control both the speed of the planets . . ."

Now the planets were moving *too* fast. They were whipping around so rapidly that they were starting to tilt away from the sun. Jeremy jiggled the lever again, but nothing happened. The planets only went faster.

People in the audience were starting to laugh, but it didn't sound like the warm, friendly laughter that Suzanne had gotten. This was more like snickering.

Totally humiliated, Jeremy switched off his model.

The planets stopped abruptly, jiggling and swinging on their nylon cords. Jeremy felt like racing offstage and hiding, but that would only make it worse.

He cleared his throat. "I'm very sorry, ladies and gentlemen," he said, trying not to let his voice crack. "But there's been some . . . ah, technical difficulty. I . . . ah, will still explain how I designed my system of gears . . ."

Somehow, Jeremy managed to get through the rest of his speech. The applause was pretty loud, considering he'd totally blown it, but Jeremy knew it was all over. There was no way he could win after what had just happened. As the curtains drew together, Jeremy wheeled his booth offstage and headed back into the exhibition hall. He felt like crying. In fact, he was afraid if he saw anyone he knew that he would do just that. That would be the final humiliation.

Jeremy considered just leaving his booth any old place for the custodians to find and dump in the trash. Then he could find a bus to take home so he wouldn't have to face his brothers or his parents. They must be so ashamed of him right now. His mother would never use the word brilliant to describe him again. In fact, as long as he was taking the bus, maybe he should take it in the opposite direction, as far away from

113

home as possible. After the way he'd disappointed his parents today, they probably wouldn't miss him one bit.

But that would be giving up. Jeremy couldn't do that. Besides, he didn't have any money for bus fare. Which left him with only one choice. He had to face his family again. And the sooner he got it over with, the sooner he could put this whole thing behind him.

Jeremy slowly wheeled his booth back to its original spot, then he headed for the entrance to the auditorium. When he stepped inside, at the back of the audience, he saw a girl in white coveralls explaining how she'd built a solar-powered go-cart. Jeremy rolled his eyes. Where were all these science whizzes last year? Jeremy had never seen projects like this in elementary school.

Moving down the aisle, Jeremy searched for his family, but the auditorium was too dark for him to see anybody clearly. He might as well just find any seat and catch up with them afterwards.

"This go-cart is built to scale," the girl in the white coveralls finished her speech. "If a full-sized car were built using the solar-powered motor I've designed, it would be able to travel for three hundred miles without recharging. Thank you."

The girl hopped into her go-cart and drove it offstage to thunderous applause. Jeremy sank into an empty seat on the aisle, hoping no one would recognize him as the guy with the lame project.

The next few hours made him feel like sinking all the way to the floor. He saw self-sustaining ecosystems, a new breed of mice created by gene splicing, and, worst of all, two other models of the solar system, only one was generated in three-dimensional images on a computer screen and the other was a free-floating system of balls that stayed suspended in midair through the use of superconducting magnets.

As the curtain closed for the last time, one of the judges, a tall man with a black mustache, appeared from behind it. "We'll have a brief break while we choose our winners," he said. "Please stay seated while we tally the scores."

Jeremy closed his eyes and heaved a deep sigh. To think all he'd been worried about was the speed control on his model. Even if his planets had spun perfectly, his project wouldn't even have come close to some of the other ones he'd seen, especially Suzanne's.

Jeremy had wanted to think Miss Wilson was playing favorites with Suzanne, but now he could see how wrong he was. Miss Wilson told Suzanne her project was wonderful because it *was*. It was obvious Suzanne had spent a long time thinking about it and putting it together. Most of the other people today had, too. They hadn't waited until the last minute, like Jeremy, then slapped something together.

Jeremy couldn't believe, now, that he'd ever been so cocky. His "elaborate system of gears" wasn't any more impressive than the gears on a cuckoo clock or a wind-up toy. How could that compare with space-age high tech inventions?

The tall judge with the black mustache reappeared from behind the curtain. "May I have your attention please?"

The audience, which had been murmuring, quieted down. Jeremy leaned his elbow on the armrest and let his cheek fall into his hand.

"We have chosen our finalists," the judge said. "We will be awarding a first, second, and third prize. The winner of our third prize, and a one-thousand-dollar scholarship, is Mark Goldenberg for his genetically engineered Splice Mice."

Everyone applauded, and a skinny boy with dark hair walked across the stage to receive an envelope from the judge.

"Second prize," the judge continued as Mark left the stage, "and a twenty-five-hundred-dollar schol-

arship is awarded to Michael Mackay for his superconducting solar system."

Jeremy could hardly bear to watch. He let his eyes
wander over the audience, looking for his family. As
he searched, he noticed Jason and Kevin Whittaker
sitting with their father. The three of them were staring silently at the stage, their faces stony. Jeremy
could tell how nervous they were, and how much they
were all hoping Suzanne would win.

The judge paused and smiled. "It wasn't easy picking a winner this year since there were so many out-
standing entries. But I am happy to announce that
this year's winner of first prize and a five-thousand-
dollar scholarship is . . ."

Jeremy sat up a little straighter. He noticed that
all three of the Whittakers did too.

"Suzanne Whittaker!" the judge said with a big
smile.

The audience cheered and hooted and yelled. The
Whittakers jumped up from their seats and pushed
through their row, running down to the stage to join
Suzanne.

Jeremy felt a little sick to his stomach, but he made
himself clap. He meant it, too. Suzanne really did
deserve it. But being beaten at all, and especially by

Suzanne Whittaker really hurt. He'd never hear the end of it. Kevin Whittaker would probably shove it in Jeremy's face for the rest of his life.

"There you are, Jeremy!" his mother said, tapping him on the arm. "We were wondering where you'd disappeared to." Jeremy's dad and brothers were standing next to her.

Jeremy swallowed hard. Hunching his shoulders, he turned to look up at his mother. "Sorry," he said simply. "I know you're disappointed in me. I don't blame you, either."

His mother smiled and held her arms open to give him a hug. Jeremy wasn't crazy about the idea of hugging his mother in public, but he was so glad his mother still loved him he stood up and let her wrap her arms around him. It also felt good to be hugged. It made him feel less like bawling.

"Well, of course we're sorry that *you're* disappointed," his mother said, "but it's not the end of the world. There's always next year."

Jeremy closed his eyes and inhaled his mother's flowery cologne. His eyes pricked. "I wanted you to think I was brilliant," he sniffled. He felt like such a baby.

"You are," his mother said. "You just didn't win, that's all."

"It's just one contest," Jeremy's dad said. "It doesn't change the way we think of you."

Jeremy broke away from his mother and looked up at his father. He blinked away the tears threatening to spill over. He might have messed up his project, but he was determined *not* to cry. "I could have tried harder," he said, with the tiniest of catches in his voice. "I could have spent more time on my project and . . . and worked more carefully."

Mr. Jenkins shrugged. "So you'll learn for next time."

"There's always next year," Lee said, shaking his bangs out of his eyes. "And you can still be a karate champ."

Jeremy felt like a complete idiot. Here he'd been wasting time feeling sorry for himself when he could have been getting all geared up for the karate demonstration.

So what if he didn't become a world-famous scientist? He was still a super athlete and possibly even a TV star. Once the news cameras started rolling tomorrow morning, he'd forget all about this stupid science fair. And, once they saw him in action, so would everyone else.

Anyway, he could still try to kick butt in next year's science fair!

Chapter Eleven

"Here we go again," Jeremy said the next morning as his dad backed the Jeep out of the driveway. Jeremy sat in the back seat, between his two brothers. All three of them were wearing fresh, white cotton karate uniforms, or gi. Lee also had a black leather carrying case on his lap which held his sai.

"It's going to go a lot better today," Jeremy's mother promised, turning around from the front passenger seat.

"Yeah," Michael said. "Don't even think about what happened yesterday. Just focus on the bunkai, and you'll do fine."

"I don't even *remember* yesterday," Jeremy insisted.

Of course, Jeremy was lying. He'd relived every moment of his humiliation at least ten times as he was trying to fall asleep, which meant he hadn't fallen asleep until four o'clock in the morning. But Jeremy was getting used to not sleeping. It had been so long since he'd had a decent night's sleep that he almost didn't remember what it was like.

Jeremy's dad turned right at the end of the street and rounded the curve past the Bonny Brook Country Club. They crossed over a main road, passed Midvale Middle School, and headed down the hill to the mall. Just past the mall, they entered downtown Midvale and reached a big municipal parking lot. The lot was almost completely filled with cars even though it was only nine o'clock on Sunday morning.

"Looks like quite a turnout," Mr. Jenkins said, glancing across the street at the town green.

Jeremy turned to look, too. The green was a broad, flat, grassy lawn, which was now covered with picnic blankets and hundreds of people strolling, standing, or sitting, waiting for the karate demonstration to begin. At the back of the lawn was a big bandshell and stage with a red curtain. Jeremy could see several white-uniformed figures up on stage talking. Then Jeremy noticed the WMID-TV news van pulled up on the grass alongside the stage. It had a little radar dish on top, and long heavy cables trailing out of the open back door.

121

Lee started tapping his feet nervously against the floor. "I can't believe all these people," he said. "I hope I don't get stage fright."

"You won't," Jeremy assured his brother, even though he felt just as nervous. He *had* to prove himself in front of Sensei, the Whittakers, his parents, the audience, and the news cameras. It was the only way he could make up for failing so miserably yesterday. Still, Lee had a lot less to be nervous about than Jeremy. He was the best student at the dojo. Did he know something Jeremy didn't?

Jeremy's dad parked the Jeep, and the family headed across the lot towards the green. The October sky was slightly overcast, and the weather was cool but comfortable. In other words, perfect karate weather.

After crossing the street, Jeremy and his brothers left their parents and jogged up the green towards the stage. Sensei Davis, dressed in his gi, was up on stage, chatting with some of the other grown-ups who were also black belts. Groups of deshi were practicing their katas in formation on the grass behind the bandshell.

A young woman wearing a baseball cap with *The Courier* emblazoned on its band wandered among them. *The Courier* was the local newspaper, and she must be their reporter. Occasionally, she would stop to ask someone a question, recording the conversation on a mini-tape recorder. Jeremy couldn't wait to join the group so the reporter would ask *him* some questions.

But Jeremy forgot all about the newspaper interviewer when he spotted Vic Vernon and the WMID-TV news camera. Vic, a tall handsome black man in his early forties, stood beneath a tree. He was talking to a chunky young woman with curly black hair who balanced a video camera on her shoulder. Vic wore an expensive-looking gray suit and a heavy gold watch, and he spoke in a deep, resonant voice. Everything about him said TV star!

Jeremy edged towards the tree, hoping Mr. Vernon would notice him. Jeremy had never met him before, but he hoped that Dwight had told his father who Jeremy was. Maybe Vic Vernon was even *looking* for Jeremy, the star of his son's bunkai. If Mr. Vernon was going to cover their demonstration properly, he'd have to get Jeremy's perspective.

Dwight broke away from a group practicing kata on the lawn and jogged towards his dad. "You ready for me yet?" he asked. Dwight's hair, always cut very short, was practically shaved into baldness. On any other kid this might have looked weird, but Dwight was cool enough to pull it off.

"Yes," Vic Vernon said, positioning Dwight beneath the tree. "Brenda, let's get a two shot."

The camerawoman moved back a few feet and focused her lens on Dwight and his father.

"Angle yourself a little," Vic instructed his son. After Dwight had turned his shoulder so he was half-facing his father, Vic nodded at Brenda. "Let's roll," he said.

"I want to hear this," Jeremy whispered to his brothers, who also seemed interested in watching the interview.

"How long have you been studying karate?" Vic asked his son.

Jeremy held back a laugh. Vic had to know the answer to that since he was the one who paid for Dwight to study karate. But Vic was probably pretending he didn't know Dwight so the interview would seem more professional.

"Two years," Dwight said, smiling into the camera. "I take four classes a week. I'd take even more if my dad would let me, but he wants to make sure I spend enough time on my homework."

Vic nodded solemnly, though Jeremy saw his mouth twitch. "I see. And tell me, how has karate changed your life?"

Jeremy waited for Dwight to make one of his usual

jokes, but Dwight's face grew serious. "It's changed my life a lot," Dwight said. "It's made me more disciplined. And it's helped me stay calm in difficult situations."

"Anything else?" Vic asked.

Dwight grinned. "It's made me a mass of muscle!" He pulled back the white sleeve of his gi and flexed his arm. "People are scared to mess with me, now. Just kidding."

"Very funny," Vic said to Dwight.

He turned to Brenda. "Was that enough?" he asked her.

"Yup, I got all the levels adjusted. Whenever you're ready to start, Vic," she told him.

Dwight's face fell. "You mean you were just kidding? That isn't gonna be on TV?" he asked.

"Come on, son, you know I can't very well pretend I don't know you," Vic told him. "How would it look if I did an exclusive interview with my own son and tried to make it look like it wasn't a set-up?" Dwight looked glum, but he nodded.

Jeremy felt a pang of alarm. Uh-oh. Did this mean he couldn't be on TV, either, since he was a friend of Dwight's?

"How about calling some of your friends over here and I'll tape a short interview with a group of you,

OK?" Vic said then to Dwight. "No guarantee it'll air, but . . ."

This was the chance Jeremy had been waiting for. "Come on!" he hissed at his brothers. "Let's go over there." Jeremy stode quickly across the grass towards Dwight. "Hey, Dwight!" he said in his friendliest tone. "How's it going?"

"You guys want to be on the news?" Dwight asked, answering Jeremy's prayers.

Jeremy tried to act casual, like this wasn't the whole reason he'd walked over. "Sure," he said. "I guess."

"These are the guys I'm doing my bunkai with," Dwight told his father. "Jeremy, Michael, and Lee Jenkins."

"Great!" Vic Vernon said. "Let's get the four of you together. Brenda, back it up a little so you can get all of us in the frame."

Jeremy was disappointed. He'd been hoping to go solo. But he could still make sure he answered most of the questions. Jeremy planted himself right in the middle of the group, in front of his brothers and Dwight.

"OK . . ." Vic started to say, but Sensei's voice rang out from the stage.

"Everybody onstage," Sensei directed. "We're ready to begin."

Talk about bad timing! Michael, Lee, and Dwight broke into a run towards the stage, but Jeremy moved much more slowly.

"We'll catch you later," Vic Vernon said. "Don't worry. I won't forget." He gave Jeremy a broad smile with his perfect white teeth.

Jeremy smiled back. "See you later!" he promised, waving as he followed the other white-uniformed people heading for the stairs on either side of the stage. Vic Vernon was a great guy. It was almost like he could read Jeremy's mind. Or maybe Vic just recognized that Jeremy was a person like himself—someone who had what it took for TV stardom, someone who was going to accomplish great things—starting today.

"Shugo! Line up!" Sensei said as the stage filled with fifty kids and adults. "Four lines, rank order," he said as Jeremy hurried up the stairs at the right of the stage. "Children in the two center lines. Adults on the outside."

Jeremy scurried to the middle of the stage and stood at attention behind Cindy Malmo, a green belt. Michael was two people ahead of him, and Lee stood at the front of the other kids' line. Down on the green, everybody sat in respectful silence.

Sensei stepped forward to a microphone. "Good

127

morning, ladies and gentlemen," he said in his raspy voice. "I'd like to welcome everyone to the third annual outdoor demonstration of the Midvale Karate Dojo. Before we start, I'd like to give you a brief history of our style of karate.

"Karate originated in the fifteenth century on the island of Okinawa, which is located halfway between China and Japan. The Okinawans, a peace-loving people, wanted to live without weapons, so they developed their own style of self-defense, *te*, which literally means 'hands.' "

Jeremy shifted ever so slightly to his right so he could see what Vic Vernon was doing. Vic and Brenda had moved around in front of the stage, and Brenda was shooting Sensei.

Brenda was now panning the deshi with her camera. Jeremy started to shift a little further to the right so his face would get in the shot, but a brown belt glared at him so he got back in line.

Sensei had taken the microphone off its stand and started walking across the stage. "Karate is based on a combination of stances, kicks, punches, and blocks," he was saying. "It emphasizes proper technique and proper breathing by practicing exercises over and over again. Most important, karate develops the *spirit* as well as the body. The karate student learns to confront his fears, to empty his mind of anger, and to focus his physical and mental energies. In short, he sees karate not as the art of self-defense but as *karate-do*—the way to greater understanding."

Loud applause filled the amphitheater, and Sensei replaced the microphone. Then he turned to face the deshi. "Sit. Seiza."

Jeremy dropped to the stage, his legs folded beneath him. After a minute of meditation, Sensei led everyone in a quick warm-up. Then he instructed the students to form a double line around the back and sides of the stage. Jeremy made sure he found a spot in the front row, center stage, so he'd be on camera as much as possible.

"We'll start with our youngest group in a demonstration of Fukyugata Ichi, the first kata," Sensei said, stepping to the side of the stage. "Shugo! Line up."

All the white belt kids ran to the center of the stage and formed two straight lines. After they performed their kata, Sensei kept them up there demonstrating basic techniques—kicks, punches, and blocks.

Jeremy fought the temptation to close his eyes. It was hard standing perfectly still for such a long time. Or maybe all those sleepless nights were finally catching up with him.

But this was no time to think of sleep. Jeremy's

turn would be coming up soon. It was time to get psyched. It didn't matter anymore what had happened yesterday. This was a new audience. Except for his parents and the Whittakers, nobody knew anything about him except that he was singlehandedly going to fight three attackers and win.

The white belts bowed and shouted "Arigato, Sensei!" Then they rejoined the other deshi at the sides of the stage.

Sensei walked back to the microphone. "Next," he announced, "we'll have a demonstration of Pinan Shodan, the first green belt kata. As I mentioned earlier, a kata is a series of choreographed movements performed against an imaginary opponent. By practicing these moves over and over again, they eventually become instinctive. If we were ever to be attacked, hopefully we would be able to use these defensive and offensive techniques without even thinking."

Come on, Jeremy silently rushed Sensei. Everything Sensei was saying was interesting, but it was taking so *long*.

"First we'll show you Pinan Shodan," Sensei said. "Then we'll show you the kata again with bunkai, meaning against actual opponents instead of imaginary ones. Jeremy Jenkins, on the spot."

Jeremy rushed forward and slammed his hands

down to his sides at attention. "Onegai-shimasu, Sensei!" he yelled, bowing smartly.

"Onegai-shimasu," Sensei answered. "Yo-i!"

Jeremy took the ready stance and waited. Down on the grass below him, Brenda aimed her camera right at him. Jeremy's first impulse was to smile, but then he decided a fierce warrior expression would be even better.

"*Hajime!*" Sensei yelled.

Jeremy began the kata, pretending Michael, Lee, and Dwight were surrounding him. He blocked. He kicked. He punched. He kiaied at the top of his lungs. By the time he was finished, he was out of breath and pretty sweaty, but he couldn't help feeling good. He'd gotten through the kata perfectly. Now he only had to do it again with bunkai, and he was home free. The audience applauded enthusiastically.

"Demonstrating bunkai are Lee Jenkins, Michael Jenkins, and Dwight Vernon," Sensei said.

Jeremy's brothers and Dwight ran to surround Jeremy. They all bowed to Jeremy and he bowed back. "Onegai-shimasu!"

"Yo-i!" Sensei commanded.

As Jeremy took the ready stance again, the other three raised their fists in front of their chests in passive fighting stance. Jeremy noticed Brenda move in closer with her camera. Then, out of the corner of his eye, he saw Kevin Whittaker, in the front row on stage, with a snide look on his face. Jeremy sneered inwardly. Kevin would be afraid to look at him like that again after this was over.

"Hajime!" Sensei called.

Jeremy whipped around in cat stance to block Michael's punch to the nose.

Crack!

The sound of their arm bones hitting each other was so sharp it made the audience gasp. Michael punched again.

Crack!

Jeremy slammed his right arm down against Michael's and countered with a punch. Then, he whipped around to block Lee's attack from the other side.

Jeremy fought off Dwight just as ferociously, turned and blocked Michael's walking punches, and screamed out a kiai as he thrust out a spear hand. This was going even better than last time. Jeremy was unbeatable!

Jeremy paused for just the briefest second to check out the look on Kevin Whittaker's face. Kevin wasn't laughing at him now. Still looking at Kevin, Jeremy started his next move, the tricky three-quarter back turn. Jeremy crossed his left foot behind him and flung his body around to meet Dwight's punch. Wait until Kevin and the camera saw this!

Maybe it was the force of Jeremy's body turning so fast. Maybe it was the drops of sweat that made the stage so slippery. Maybe Jeremy's balance was off from lack of sleep. Or maybe it was the fact that he was looking at Kevin instead of snapping his head around in the direction he was turning.

Jeremy had plenty of time to think about it afterwards, but it all happened in a split second. Jeremy whipped around, slipped, and fell with a loud thump right on his butt.

The only sound louder than the thump was the ripple of laughter. It wasn't just from the audience, either. Some of the kids onstage were giggling, and even some of the adult deshi were smiling. Worst of all, the news camera was still rolling, recording every second of Jeremy's humiliation.

Lee and Michael leaned down to help Jeremy up.

"You okay?" Michael asked. "Do you want to keep going?"

Jeremy wasn't badly hurt. He knew the smartest thing would be to keep going. But he'd had enough.

He couldn't bear one more second of feeling like the world's biggest fool. Without a word to anyone, Jeremy stood up slowly and carefully. Then he strode offstage. He took off across the green, into downtown Midvale, and kept on running, his bare feet slapping against the concrete sidewalk.

Chapter Twelve

"Jeremy!" his mother called up the stairs for the third time. "Don't you want any supper?"

Jeremy sat on his bed, his back against the sloping wall, staring at his bookshelf. He'd been sitting like this all afternoon, ever since his dad had run after him down Main Street and driven him home. Of course, his dad hadn't taken him home right away. He'd tried to talk Jeremy into going back to the demonstration.

You know what they say about falling off a horse, his dad had said. You've got to climb right back on again.

But this was much worse than falling off a horse because everyone in town had been there to see it. And everyone in the whole county was there to see it yesterday when he messed up at the science fair.

There was no way he could face anyone ever again. In fact, Jeremy had already thought of ten persuasive arguments to convince his dad to move the family to another state.

"Jeremy!" his mom called again. "I swear you'll like it. I ordered a pizza, double cheese with pepperoni."

Jeremy's mouth started to water. His mother must have really felt sorry for him, because she'd ordered his favorite food in the entire world. But Jeremy couldn't come downstairs yet. Lee and Michael were there. They had to be furious with him not just for falling down but also for abandoning them on stage. They must have felt pretty stupid standing up there with no one to fight.

"No thanks," Jeremy shouted through his locked door.

Jeremy knew he was being a coward. But being a coward was nothing compared to all the other things he was. He was lazy for not thinking of a better science project. He was a klutz for slipping and falling in front of everyone. And he was a jerk for bragging to everyone when he had nothing to brag about.

Jeremy had tried to find someone else to blame for what had happened, but the only person he'd come up with was himself. He'd ignored everybody's warnings that he was trying to do too much in too short a time. He'd been too sure of himself. He'd thought he was so much smarter and stronger than everybody else that he didn't have to give his best effort.

He'd been wrong, and now he deserved to suffer for it. He deserved to stay in his room forever. He deserved to starve to death.

A piece of notepaper slid beneath Jeremy's door. Curious, Jeremy got off his bed, reached down to pick it up, and unfolded it. The note said:

> *There's a slice of pizza outside your door. You don't have to eat it if you don't want to.*
>
> *Love, Mom*

Come to think of it, there was a deliciously spicy smell in the air. With the pizza just a door away, it was hard to resist. Quietly unlocking his door, Jeremy opened it a crack and peered out.

The upstairs hall was empty except for a plate on the floor with a steaming, melty slice of pizza on it, dotted with glistening red circles of pepperoni.

Well, as long as he didn't have to see anybody . . .

Jeremy grabbed the plate and started to close the door again, but he overheard his name being said downstairs. Jeremy knew his family could only be criticizing him behind his back, but he forced himself to listen. No matter how bad it was, he had to hear

it. It was time he saw himself for what he really was—
a total loser.

"Keep the sound down real low," Lee was saying.
"That way Jeremy won't hear it."

"I still want to tape it, though," Michael said.

Folding his pizza slice and stuffing half of it in his
mouth, Jeremy took a few steps out into the hall so
he could hear more.

Fast-paced, electronic music jingled on the TV
downstairs, and Jeremy had his answer. It was the
six o'clock local news. Vic Vernon's report on the
karate demonstration would be on any minute.

Jeremy wanted to run back to his room and lock
the door again. But he couldn't hide forever. And once
he faced his final humiliation—seeing his fall on the
news—life could only get better. Swallowing his last
few bites of pizza, Jeremy crept down the stairs and
peeked into the living room.

No one noticed him, at first. His parents sat on the
turquoise sofa amid the pink and purple pillows his
mother loved and everyone else hated. His brothers
sat on the white carpet at their parents' feet. The
large-screen TV glowed in the middle of the room.

Without a word to anyone, Jeremy sat on the floor
beside the sofa.

"Jeremy!" his mother cried, instantly reaching for the remote control.

"No, Mom," Jeremy said. "It's okay. Leave it on."

Vic Vernon's familiar face appeared on the screen. A pretty Asian anchorwoman sat next to him. Jeremy barely paid attention as they ran through stories of a local fire, a robbery in a jewelry store, and the results of the school board elections. But then, on the little square panel above Vic's left shoulder, an illustration of a boy and girl in karate uniforms appeared, and Vic started talking about the karate demonstration.

Jeremy clutched his knees to his chest as Vic's face was replaced by video footage of the event. As Vic's voice narrated, Jeremy saw Kevin Whittaker, screwing up his face as he kiaied doing first kata. He didn't look half-bad, considering he was just a white belt. There was Lee doing his sai kata like an expert. Then Sensei Davis broke a brick with each fist.

Everybody looked good. Jeremy began to feel a glimmer of hope that Vic had decided not to use the footage of him after all. Maybe Vic just wanted to show people who knew what they were doing. But then Jeremy saw the image of a boy with bright red hair wearing a green belt and a smug expression. As Vic Vernon talked about the "agony of defeat," Jeremy watched the boy splat onto the stage, his legs flying up in the air.

The karate footage ended, and the sports reporter came on to talk about the high school football game, but Jeremy still saw the image of his fall repeating itself over and over in his mind. Even if Michael hadn't been taping it on the VCR, Jeremy knew he'd never forget this as long as he lived. But maybe that was good. Maybe the memory would stop him from acting like such a jerk in the future.

Rrrrring! Rrrrring!

The cordless phone warbled, and Jeremy's mother leaned over to the end table to pick it up. "It's for you," she told Jeremy, handing him the receiver.

"Jeremy?" said the boy on the other end. Jeremy recognized Dwight's voice. "I'm calling to apologize."

"What for?" Jeremy asked. "I'm the one who should apologize to you for running off the stage."

"So we weren't exactly the hit of the show," Dwight said. "Big deal. But that's no excuse for my dad putting it on the air. It wasn't him, actually, who edited the video. My dad got called away from the demonstration to cover the fire. By the time he got back to the studio, the producer had put your fall in, and it was too late to change it."

"It's nice of you to feel bad," Jeremy said, "but it's

my own fault. If I hadn't fallen, they wouldn't have been able to put it on TV. And tell your dad not to feel bad either," Jeremy said.

"Okay," Dwight said, sounding relieved. "See you in karate class tomorrow?"

Jeremy hesitated. "Uh, maybe," he said. "Thanks for calling. 'Bye."

Jeremy turned the phone off and stared unseeingly at the TV screen. Dwight had brought up the one thing Jeremy was most afraid of. Jeremy had thought he'd be a champion. Stardom in karate movies was only a phone call away. But after the way he'd embarrassed Sensei and the school, Sensei might not let Jeremy set foot in the dojo ever again.

After locking his bicycle the next afternoon, Jeremy peered through the dojo's plate glass window. It was three o'clock. The kids' class didn't start for another half hour, but already there were a bunch of kids in their gi warming up on the deck or practicing kata. A bunch of lucky kids who knew they could study karate for as long as they wanted without the fear of getting kicked out.

"Are you going to stand there all day?" Michael asked as he pulled open the glass door. "Why don't you come in?"

"In a minute," Jeremy said as Michael and Lee entered the dojo. Jeremy squinted through the window, trying to see if he could make out Sensei among the white uniforms. If only Jeremy could take a look at Sensei's face, he might be able to get an idea of what kind of mood Sensei was in. If he looked angry, then Jeremy wouldn't even bother to go in. But Jeremy didn't see Sensei anywhere. Cautiously, Jeremy opened the door and stepped inside the long front hall, which ran from left to right.

"Hello, Jeremy," Sensei said. He was standing in the doorway to his office, at the left end of the hallway. He wasn't wearing his gi but instead wore a red polo shirt and khaki pants. Even in street clothes, though, he looked like a powerful fighter.

Jeremy swallowed. It was impossible to sneak up on Sensei, but Sensei always was able to catch him by surprise.

Sensei retreated into his office and gestured for Jeremy to follow him. "I'd like to speak to you a minute," he said.

Jeremy had no choice but to obey. If he didn't, Sensei would be even angrier. Then Jeremy would *definitely* get kicked out of the dojo. Jeremy's only chance now was to be on his best behavior.

"Sit down," Sensei said, stepping behind a battered brown desk and sitting down.

Jeremy sat on a straight-backed wooden chair and stared above Sensei's head at the wall full of black-and-white photographs of karate students from years past. He wasn't really looking at the pictures, but he was trying to distract himself so he wouldn't look too scared.

"So," Sensei said pleasantly, "how was your science fair? It was this weekend, wasn't it?"

Jeremy's eyes met Sensei's dark brown ones. The science fair was the last thing he'd expected Sensei to talk about. Jeremy was surprised a busy man like Sensei even remembered the science fair.

"Uh . . . the fair was fine," Jeremy mumbled. "At least, the other people's exhibits were. Mine wasn't so great, though."

"Oh?" Sensei asked, rolling back a little in his cushioned desk chair.

"Actually," Jeremy admitted, "mine was one of the worst. I didn't put enough time and effort into it."

Sensei nodded and folded his massive arms across his chest. "I'm not surprised. I'm not surprised about what happened at the karate demonstration, either."

Jeremy's heart lurched in his chest. He shouldn't

143

have been fooled by Sensei's friendly tone. Sensei was about to lay into him for making the whole dojo look bad.

"I had a feeling you weren't going to do too well in your bunkai," Sensei said, his voice as pleasant as before.

Jeremy waited for more, but Sensei sat there silently. Was that it? Jeremy was confused.

"If you knew I wasn't going to do well," Jeremy ventured, "then how come you let me be in the demonstration? Why didn't you just kick me out beforehand?"

"But that was the point," Sensei said, smiling. "That's exactly why I allowed you to continue."

"Because you knew I'd mess up?"

Sensei nodded.

Now Jeremy was *really* confused. Why would Sensei purposely ruin his own karate demonstration in front of the whole town? "I don't get it," Jeremy said.

Sensei leaned forward in his chair and rested his arms on the desk. "There's an old Japanese proverb," he said. " 'A hunter who chases two rabbits at the same time will catch neither of them.' " Sensei stared at Jeremy with his inky dark eyes.

Slowly, Sensei's meaning began to dawn on Jeremy. "You mean *I'm* the hunter?" he asked. "And the science fair and the demonstration were my two rabbits?"

Sensei nodded. "It's a lesson most of us need to learn at some point," he said. "And learning it was just as much a part of your karate training as kata or bunkai."

"But I ruined the demonstration!" Jeremy exclaimed. "Aren't you mad?"

"You didn't ruin it," Sensei said. "It was embarrassing for you, but most people hardly thought about it afterwards. Things like that are never as important to anyone else as they are to us, but that's another lesson."

Jeremy was starting to breathe a little easier. If his falling down was just another karate lesson, then maybe Sensei wasn't going to kick him out after all. Maybe Sensei was saying it was OK to be wrong about something, as long as you learned from it.

Jeremy thought back to the quote he'd read on Sensei's bulletin board, the one by Bruce Lee. "The less effort, the faster and more powerful you will be." Jeremy smiled as he finally realized what that quote meant. It didn't mean "Don't try your best." It meant "Don't try *too* hard." If Jeremy hadn't been trying so hard to impress Kevin Whittaker and show off for the cameras, he probably wouldn't have fallen down.

Jeremy remembered, too, the day he'd nearly passed out. He'd thought Sensei was complimenting him for being a fast learner. What Sensei had really been saying was that Jeremy was rushing through his kata *too* fast.

"I guess I've got a lot of lessons to learn," Jeremy said, sitting up a little straighter in his seat. "I've got to calm down and focus on one thing at a time. But I guess I learned this a little too late."

"Why do you say that?" Sensei asked.

"The demonstration's over," Jeremy said. "I'll never be able to undo what I did wrong."

"But that doesn't mean you won't get another chance," Sensei said. "There's another demonstration six months from now. You can start practicing for that."

Jeremy tried not to look too hopeful. "You'd let me be in it, even after what happened yesterday?"

"As long as you keep learning," Sensei said. "No matter how advanced you get in karate or in life, you should always be learning."

Sensei pulled open the top drawer of his desk and pulled out a pen and a white index card. Then he wrote something on the card. "Here," Sensei said, handing the card to Jeremy. "You can put this up on the bulletin board."

Jeremy nodded. Here was one lesson he understood right away. The card said:

Karate is a lifetime marathon.
                                              —*Shosin Nagamine*

Glossary

Arigato—Thank you

Bo—Weapon. Wooden staff with tapered ends

Bunkai—Application of kata where one or more actual opponents demonstrate attacking techniques

Cat stance—Body weight rests on the bent back leg. Front foot lightly touches the floor. Most advantageous position for attacking an opponent's side

Chasing punch—Used with wide, open-leg stance to deliver blow to opponent's chest by extending the fist sideward

Deshi—Karate student (below black belt level)

Dojo—Sacred hall of learning; Karate school

Doshokai—Meeting

Dozo—Please

Fukyugata Ichi—First white belt kata composed of

walking and reverse punches, down blocks, and high blocks. Most basic kata

Gi—Karate uniform

Hajime—Begin

Karate—Weaponless form of self-defense. Literally means "Empty (*kara*) hand (*te*)"

Karate-do—The "way" of Karate. Karate as more than a martial art but a philosophy, a way of life

Kata—Form. An organized series of pre-arranged defensive and offensive movements symbolizing an imaginary fight between several opponents and performed in a geometrical pattern. Handed down and perfected by masters of a system of karate

Kiai—Concentration of energy and power in one sharp burst, sometimes accompanied by a loud shout used to startle opponent

Knife hands—Four fingers straight and pressed stiffly together. Thumb pressed in tightly. Side of hand used to slash or strike an opponent

Makiwara—Striking post, used to toughen knuckles and hands

Mawate—Turn

Naihanchi Sho—First brown belt kata. Features

wide-legged "horse" stance. Trains lower parts of the body

Nunchuku—Flail (a weapon). Two wooden sticks connected by a rope

Onegai-shimasu—Please teach me

Pinan Nidan—Second green belt kata

Pinan Shodan—First green belt kata. Introduces cat stance and knife hand techniques

Reverse punch—Punching fist is opposite side of forward leg

Rei—Bow

Sai—Slender, pointed weapon, resembling a sword

Samurai—Japanese warrior

Seiza—Folded leg sitting position

Sempai—Senior student

Sensei—Teacher or master

Shinden—Old masters, ancient and past teachers of Karate

Shotu-mate—Stop; be quiet

Shugo—Line up

Solar plexus—Nerve center located beneath the rib cage. A vulnerable target

Spear hand—Fingers straight and pressed tightly together, thumb pressed in tight. Fingertips used to thrust at eyes, solar plexus, or ribs

Te—Hand

Walking punch—Punching fist is same side as forward leg

Yo-i—Ready

COUNTING

Ichi—One

Ni—Two

San—Three

Shi—Four

Go—Five

Roku—Six

Shichi—Seven

Hachi—Eight

Ku—Nine

Ju—Ten

JOHN